THE MAGNOLIA INN

THE RED STILETTO BOOK CLUB SERIES

ANNE-MARIE MEYER

1

MAGGIE

And there it was.

Eye level and taped on all four corners. Whoever had put it there meant business and wanted me to see it. And they'd succeeded.

The notice was smaller than I'd expected. And oranger. I snorted.

I'd never had an eviction notice cemented to my door before, so what did I know? I'd also never been divorced and had my entire bank account drained by the man who'd sworn to love me forever.

Apparently my thirty-sixth year was the year fate decided to land all the blows it could. I was divorced, penniless, and now—homeless.

I cursed under my breath as I fought the tears that stung my eyes. In my slow descent into madness, I didn't notice Mrs. Jacamo, my nosy and judgy neighbor, until she stepped around me. She tsked, lowered her head, and scurried by. She was carrying her dog, Baby, in a bag that was tucked under her armpit. I could see his black eyes stare at me as she retreated.

I thought for a moment that Baby had it worse than me. Living in her owner's armpit had to be bad—but with one more look at the note taped to my door, I dropped that thought.

I had it worse.

I grabbed the piece of paper, crumpled it in my hand, and shoved my key into the lock. I fought back the tears as I turned the handle and slipped into my apartment.

It had started out as *our* apartment, Sean's and mine, but ever since Sean packed up his belongings and left with Tracy—my now ex-friend—it had become *my* apartment.

In a few short weeks it wouldn't even be that.

I threw my purse and computer bag on the table and pulled out my phone. I sent a quick SOS text to Brielle, my best friend and designated cheerleader. She texted a thumbs-up and then an ETA of five minutes.

I set my phone on the charger and busied myself with making some coffee. Since I couldn't afford fresh coffee grounds, I had to resort to buying the instant crap that tasted bitter and chalky.

By the time Brielle banged on my door, the coffee had cooled to a sippable temperature. I held my mug in my hand as I walked over to the door and pulled it open. Brielle's face peeked up over two brown bags packed full of Cheng's to-die-for Chinese.

"Bri, you didn't have to bring food," I said as I took the six-pack of wine coolers that dangled from her fingers.

She shrugged as she followed me into the kitchen and set the bags down on the counter. "They'd just dropped it off when you texted." She began to open the bags and took out the small white containers.

The smell of sweet and sour chicken and fried rice had my mouth watering.

"Besides, I ordered too much. Brent was going to come over for dinner, but he got held up at work." She finished unloading the bag and blew her dark-brown curls from her face. "So I figured you could use some sustenance."

I reached out and pulled Brielle into a hug. She always seemed to know just what I needed. "Thanks," I said as my control on my emotions slipped, causing my voice to come out in a whisper.

She chuckled as she pointed to the cupboard. "Plates," she said.

I nodded and fished them out. One was a pale yellow and the other had flowers painted on one side. They were the perfect representation of my current status: disjointed and mismatched.

I swallowed as I focused on grabbing two plastic forks from a drawer and handing one over to Brielle. There was no way I was going to look at the status of my dishware like a Rorschach test. I didn't need an inkblot to tell me what I already knew.

My life was one giant failure that I couldn't get out from underneath. No matter how hard I tried.

Once our plates were overflowing with food, I grabbed a wine cooler and made my way over to the faded floral couch in the far corner. I settled down on it as Brielle followed and did the same.

We ate in silence for a few minutes before Brielle sighed and turned toward me. I could see the questions she had for me. They were written in her gaze.

Knowing I couldn't go the entire evening without an explanation for the SOS, I tucked my straight blonde hair behind my ear and faced her.

"I got a note today," I said after I swallowed the bit of sweet and sour chicken I'd been chewing.

Brielle raised her eyebrows and got a mischievous look on her face. "A sexy note?" she asked.

I shook my head. "Ew, no. Who would write me anything like that?" The ink on my divorce papers wasn't even dry. Six months was way too soon to start testing the waters once more.

In fact, I doubted that I would want to dip my toe into the dating pool ever again. When you are nearing forty, that water is black and murky with all kinds of ungodly things swimming around in it.

My one experience with online dating had ended horribly. My date had shown up drunk, with his earlier date on his arm. It ended with me calling a ride and slipping out through the bathroom window.

From then on, I swore that I would never let Brielle convince me to join any sort of dating app. Ever.

"Margaret Brown, you are a sexy, available girl. You

shouldn't let one bad date turn you off from a lifetime of fun." She speared her mushroom chicken with her fork and slipped it into her mouth. She raised her eyebrows as she studied me.

I waved away her comment. It wasn't just one bad date. It was one messy divorce followed by one bad date. I doubted I should test my luck again. Apparently fate was still pissed off at me for something, even if I wasn't sure what *it* was. I figured I'd take my time to ease back into her good graces.

I'd already told Brielle these theories, but she'd responded by telling me I was crazy and that there was no such thing as fate. If there was, fate would be holding seances against Sean, not me. He had his day coming where karma would catch up to him. It was only a matter of time.

Then she would end with telling me how beautiful I was and how any guy would be lucky to have me.

Ten years ago, that might have been true. But age and a dysfunctional marriage had taken its toll on my body—namely my hips. They got rounder and wider with each passing year.

"Thanks, but no, that wasn't the kind of note I got." Glancing around, I found the crumpled-up notice that I'd chucked into the corner. It was nestled in the jumbled mess of cords beside the side table. I set my plate down on the floor and walked over to pick up the paper.

I opened it and smoothed it out on my leg. Then I handed it to Brielle.

She took it, and a moment later, she gasped. I could feel her blue eyes as they stared at me. Not wanting to verify what I already knew—that I was, in fact, a loser—I settled back on the couch, with my plate balanced on my thighs, and stared at my remaining food.

"What are you going to do?" she asked.

I shrugged as I continued eating. "I need to find a job that actually pays." Working as an intern at Jacobson's Designs was my dream, but without a paycheck, it was becoming a nightmare. Even so, I seemed physically incapable of letting it go. In my stubbornness after the divorce, I'd figured I'd be able to make it work. But apparently, I'd been foolish. The funds in my bank account never increased past the double digits, and I couldn't bring myself to admit that Sean had stolen this last bit of my happiness from me. Forcing me to give up my dream because of him. Again.

My throat felt tight with each swallow, and I couldn't stop the hopelessness that was slowly suffocating me. I felt empty inside, and maybe I was hoping the food would fill it up. I guess there are worse things to bury myself in.

"Do you need to live with me?" Brielle asked. Her eyes were wide, and I could see her concern etched on her features.

I appreciated her gesture, but it wasn't even possible. She was already sharing her studio apartment with Jasmine, the granola foodie who didn't believe in showers or washing her clothes. There was no way I could fit in there as well. It was the curse of living in New York. Affordable real estate was hard to come by.

I shook my head as I tucked my feet underneath me and set my plate on my knees. "You don't have the room."

Brielle paused before she nodded and glanced around. "What about your mom?"

I almost swallowed my tongue at the mention of my mother. Penny Brown didn't take handouts—not like she needed them—and she certainly didn't give them. She believed everyone needed to earn their way in the world. Even her only daughter.

"That's a big fat no," I said, shoveling more food into my mouth. I hated that my emotions spiked at the mention of my estranged mother. It sucked.

"But she's your mom. She owes you."

I shook my head more fervently this time. I didn't want to talk about her. I didn't want to entertain the thought of asking her to help. What if I did and she turned me down?

There was a reason why I'd chosen to live with my dad when they divorced. He was warm and cuddly. Penny was cold and distant. There were times I wondered if she held my choice to stay with Dad against me. And in my booze-filled moments, I wondered what our relationship would have been like if she actually liked me.

My stomach ached, so I stopped eating and set my plate down on the floor next to me. I grabbed a nearby throw pillow and curled up with it. I laid my head on the back of the couch and peered over at Brielle.

She was poking around at her food, not really eating any of it. I could tell she was mulling things over. She wanted to find a solution. It was sweet, but she needed to face the truth just like I did.

There was no solution.

"I hear the Branson House is nice," I mumbled.

Brielle's gaze snapped over at me. "No. Nope. Nuh-uh. There is no way my best friend is staying in a shelter." She leaned into me as she shook her finger in my direction. "You are one of New York's best interior designers. You had so much potential until that loser Sean convinced you otherwise."

She stood and began to pace in front of me. "You can't give up that dream. Maybe working for Jacobson's Designs is dumb, but there has to be something more."

I sighed as I reached down and collected my plate and then Brielle's. I brought them into the kitchen, where I began to spray them off. "It's not going to happen, Brielle. I just need to find something that pays." I stared at the food as it slipped off the plate and down the drain.

It's a sad day when you find yourself relating to food as it's discarded.

"But that's the thing. What if you found both?"

I blinked as I glanced over to see Brielle standing next to me. She had both hands pressed onto the counter in front of her and she was leaning toward me with wide eyes.

"I'm sorry, what? In what universe does something like that exist?"

Brielle leaned back, folding her arms across her chest. "Listen, I write grant proposals all the time. I can help you write a proposal."

I studied her. "Who would I be writing a proposal to? And for what?"

She studied me. I could see the excitement that she was trying to hold back. She knew me so well. I was risk averse. Especially after Sean.

She paused as she stared at me, tapping her fingers on her forearm. "A proposal for your design company." She said each word slowly. Her eyebrows rose as she waited for me to respond.

I turned off the water and then faced her. "Are you talking about Studio Red? Bri, come on. That was a ridiculous dream I had years ago."

Brielle raised her finger up to silence me and then turned and marched down the hallway. I scrambled to catch up with her. I knew where she was going. I knew what binder she was looking for.

But nothing I did stopped her. She marched right into my room and located that ridiculous dream binder I'd created years ago. Back when I felt like the world was my oyster. Back when I was happy.

"This isn't a ridiculous dream. If it was, you wouldn't have kept this for so long." She settled down on my bed and flipped it open. She began to read the business proposal I'd written. It was complete with yearly projections and a business motto.

"I want to design beautiful living at affordable

prices," she read as she pointed her finger at the page and tapped it a few times. "Maggie, you loved this dream until Sean stole it from you. He's a loser who's out of your life. Maybe dreaming big is what you should do now."

She closed the binder and set it on my nightstand. "This is your do-over. How are you going to change things? The world is open to you." She stood and rested her hands on my shoulders. "Don't let fear keep you down. That's what it's done for the last ten years." She met my gaze and held it.

I wanted to tease her and tell her she sounded like those ridiculous motivational posters people buy, but I couldn't. Tears were brimming my eyelids as I stared at her. She was right. I'd been living in fear for way too long. Fear that I'd disappoint Sean. Fear that I would succeed where he'd failed. Fear that I would never be good enough for him or for myself.

Fear was a dark and sticky world. Once you got there, it was hard to leave. It clung to you and didn't let you go.

I broke her hold on me as I flopped down on the bed. I stared up at the ceiling and blew out my breath. Brielle did the same, her elbow resting next to mine.

I closed my eyes and allowed myself to imagine what my life would be like if I said yes. What if I didn't go back to Jacobson's Designs? And what if I didn't take a job at the local grocery store that seemed to always shove a *Now Hiring* flyer into my hand every time I left?

"Can you see it?" she asked.

I peeked over at her and then shrugged. "What am I supposed to see?"

"Maggie," she groaned as she grabbed a pillow and whacked me with it. "You're impossible."

I shielded my face from any further attacks. Thankfully, my sadness had erupted into giggles. I'd cried so much over Sean, I didn't think I could do it again.

Brielle must have grown tired of me and scooted to lean against my headboard. I rolled onto my side and propped my head up with my hand as I drew circles on the comforter in front of me.

I glanced up at her. "Okay. Tell me your plan, and I'll tell you if you're crazy or not."

A slow smile began to spread across her lips as she leaned forward and rubbed her hands together.

I knew I should have taken her excitement as a warning sign. A big, blinking neon-red sign that said *Run Now*. But I didn't.

After all, what other plan did I have?

I'd already messed up my life so much, what was another few years traveling down the wrong path? At least this time, it would only be me.

This time, I wouldn't have a deadweight named Sean around my neck telling me I wasn't good enough for anything.

I was starting my new life with someone who was telling me I could do it, and that was heads above where I'd been before. If Brielle was excited and confident, I'd lean on that for a while.

I was desperate. So, for right now, I'd play along.

2

CLEMENTINE

A loud, brash noise startled me from my dream. Well, *dream* was a stretch. More like a nightmare. One I'd had before. One where I was wandering the aisles of Magnolia Hardware, looking for a Phillips screwdriver—the very one I remembered stocking that morning—only to find myself lost in a maze.

No matter which turn I took, there was another long and dark path in front of me.

This nightmare was comical considering I'd lived above the hardware store my whole life. I'd grown up here. I knew this store like the back of my hand.

But that didn't seem to save me in the nightmare. I couldn't get out of the store, no matter how hard I tried.

I pushed my long, dark hair from my face as I reached over to grab my phone from the nightstand. The alarm was beeping, and the lights were flashing. Five fifteen. Time to get up.

I slid the alarm off and set my phone back down. Then I swung my feet over the side of my bed and wiggled my toes into my slippers. I flicked my hair over my shoulder and stood.

Dad would be up soon, and if I didn't beat him to the coffee pot, I'd have to dig out, yet again, whatever he'd put into the machine thinking it was coffee grounds.

One day it was flour. The next, powdered cleaner.

Shuffling over to the bathroom, I threw my hair up into a messy bun, grabbed my robe, and slipped out of my room and into the hallway. Even though I always hoped Dad would sleep in, it didn't matter. He was up every day at five thirty, ready for work, even if he couldn't remember who he was or where he was. Or that he was my dad.

I swallowed as an ache rose up inside of me.

The doctor had said it was normal. Dad's internal clock hadn't changed even if his mind had. The strong, dedicated man he'd once been was still there, even if Alzheimer's was slowly taking his memories away.

I cleared my throat, trying to dislodge the emotions that had taken up residence there. As I passed by the living room, I heard the very familiar snore of Archer. He was my older brother by four years, but lately, he was acting like a moody teenage boy.

Apparently, he hadn't had the energy to make it the rest of the way to his room—thirty feet away. Instead, he'd preferred to lay on the couch with his head cricked by the armrest and his leg draped over the back.

I rolled my eyes as I shuffled over to the couch and flung his leg off the back. It caused enough momentum to flip him off the couch and onto the floor.

A slur of curse words followed as Archer pushed his hands and knees underneath him and staggered to his feet.

"What the…Clem?" he asked, pushing his dark, curly hair away from his face. He glared at me.

That man needed a haircut and a life coach.

"Dad's going to be up soon, and you know it upsets him when he finds your *boots* on his couch," I said, pointing to his dark-brown and covered-with-mud work boots.

Archer glanced down and then back up. He shrugged as he shoved his hands into the front pockets of his jacket. "It's not like it's an expensive couch or anything. Dad's had it since they picked us up at the foster home."

I stared at him, making a point to drop my jaw so he knew exactly how I felt about what he'd said. "Seriously, Archer? What's wrong with you?" I asked as I leaned forward and brushed my hand against the pillows. Sand flung up around me, and I narrowed my eyes. Archer just stood there with an apathetic expression on his face.

"I was at a work site yesterday. I'm sorry that we live on an island that is literally surrounded by sand."

I snorted as I fluffed the pillows and then turned back to him. "Work site? What work site?" I tapped my chin with my finger. "Oh, I know. The one that starts with The Anchor Point and ends with Pub?" I glared at my brother.

I could still smell the alcohol on his clothes, his hair, and his breath.

Archer shrugged as he ran his hands through his hair. "Am I supposed to apologize for trying to have a good time?" He wandered into the kitchen, where he flipped on the water and tipped his head to the side, leaning down with his mouth open.

I growled as I marched over to him and grabbed a glass from the cupboard. I handed it over. "Seriously? It's like you were born in a barn."

Archer flipped the water off and straightened, making a point to wipe his lips in a dramatic fashion. "We could have been. Did you ever think of that?"

I growled, but he just shrugged, kicked off his boots, and threw them in the direction of the front door. "I'm going back to bed," he said as he shoved his hands into his jacket pockets and dipped his head.

I had half a mind to call after him. To tell him exactly what I thought of him. But that would only invite him to stay, and right now, arguing with my hurting brother was the last thing I wanted. Especially since Dad was due up any minute now.

"The store opens at ten. I expect you to be down there at a quarter till," I called at Archer's retreating back.

He raised his hand and gave me a mock salute as he slipped into his room and shut the door.

I took in a deep, cleansing breath and then blew it out through my mouth.

Archer wasn't a bad guy, even if he was acting like a prick. He hadn't always been this drunken shell of a man. He used to have goals and ambitions. He graduated valedictorian, complete with a full-ride to Yale. When he finished law school, he landed a job with one of New York's top law firms.

Things had been going Archer's way—until the accident. The one that took his daughter's life and, eventually, destroyed his marriage.

That's when he'd folded in on himself. It was hard, watching my brother destroy his life. To lose all desire to live. To love.

To have no motivation to do anything other than drink and fight.

I scrubbed my face with my hands, making sure to apply extra pressure around my eyes. I could feel a tension headache starting up, and I didn't have the time or patience required to nurse myself back to health.

Dad couldn't take care of things if I was sick, and Archer couldn't be bothered to pull his weight. I doubted he would even come down at ten. I'd be lucky if he sauntered into the store before two.

I was alone. Alone in taking care of my father and alone in running the store.

"No pity," I said under my breath as I made my way into the kitchen and turned on the faucet. Then I grabbed the coffee pot, filled it up, and scooped some grounds into the machine.

While that hummed to life, I pulled some eggs from the fridge and set them next to the stove. I grabbed a pan from the cupboard next to me and set it on the burner.

Dad required two fried eggs and two pieces of toast every morning. He would sit at the table, read the paper, and sip on his coffee.

Sure, there were days when I wouldn't know who I was going to get when Dad came strolling out of his room. And most days I feared that he wouldn't come out at all.

But one thing never changed: Dad's morning ritual.

While the eggs were frying, I slipped two pieces of bread into the toaster and pressed the lever down. Then I grabbed the butter and opened it.

The sound of Dad's door creaking open caused me to glance down the hall. Dad had emerged. He was in his usual jeans and button-down shirt. His hair was combed to the side and slathered with gel. His glasses were perched on his nose, and when his gaze landed on me, his smile widened.

He was older than most dads. Archer and I had been adopted when they were in their late forties. They were the perfect parents. Kind, understanding, and there for Archer and me in a way that other adults hadn't ever been. We were lucky to be saved by them.

"Good morning, Janet," he said as he walked over to me and placed a kiss on my cheek.

I winced as he called me by my mother's name. So, it

was going to be that kind of morning. "Hey, Dad," I said as I linked arms with him.

Dad stared at me with his brow furrowed. "Dad?" he asked.

I led him over to the table and pulled out his chair. "I'm not Janet, Dad. I'm Clementine, your daughter."

Dad took a seat and turned to look at me. "You're my daughter?" he asked.

I hated how confused he looked. I would give anything to bring my dad back. The giant of a man who wasn't scared of anything. Who loved to make me laugh and helped me feel safe no matter what.

A stark difference from the man sitting in front of me, looking as if he couldn't quite process what I'd told him.

The popping of eggs drew me from my thoughts, and I rushed over to pull the pan off the burner. Not wanting them to cook anymore, I slipped the eggs onto a plate. Then I pulled the toast from the toaster, wincing as I burned the tips of my fingers in the process.

I blew on them, trying to take the sting out of my skin. Then I rubbed my fingertips on the towel next to me before focusing in on buttering the toast.

Once the food was ready and his coffee poured, I brought the plate over and set it down in front of Dad.

"Love you," I said as I kissed him on the top of his head.

Dad mumbled as he took a bite of his toast. I busied myself with getting his pills and making sure that he swallowed them. Then I told him to sit tight because I would be right back.

I pulled my jacket off the hook and slipped my arms through the sleeves. I held the zipper together as I padded down the stairs and over to the back door.

Thankfully, Jacob had delivered the newspaper already. It was sitting half propped up on the exterior wall. Bending down, I picked it up and then glanced around.

The sun was barely coming up. The sky was streaked with light purples and oranges. I paused, taking in a deep breath of crisp, salty air. It was late March, and the weather was finally warming up. A familiar ache settled in my stomach as I closed my eyes.

I loved Magnolia, Rhode Island. I loved the sunrises and the smells that came from living here. I loved how this was my home and I always felt safe.

But there were times, in the quiet of the morning or the stillness of the sunset, that I wished I'd taken my chance to leave this place. The chance to dance at Juilliard, like I'd always dreamed of doing. To finally live my life like I wanted to. Like the fire inside of me begged me to do. But my mind had never allowed me to act on it.

Blowing out my breath, I forced that desire deep down in my chest where it belonged and turned, making my way back into the store. I shut the door and made my way up the stairs. Back to the reality of my life.

Dad was diagnosed my senior year of high school. At first, it was manageable, especially with Mom around. He knew he was going to get worse but had been able to keep things at bay.

But then Mom passed away and he began to forget. I came home from college every weekend to help him. Despite the community rallying to watch out for him, he got worse. I would get calls about him wandering the streets of Magnolia in search of his home, completely forgetting what day it was or where he was going.

That's when I knew I could never leave. I had to stay. So I did. I turned down Juilliard and my dreams for the future.

And here I was, ten years later, thirty-three, and working at a hardware store.

Feeling guilty for wanting something different, I forced a smile and opened up the door to the small upstairs apartment.

Dad was still sitting at the table, staring off into the distance as he methodically chewed his food.

"I have the paper," I said, setting it down in front of him and giving him a kiss. Then I wandered over to the fridge and grabbed a yogurt.

"Thank you," Dad called after me.

I nodded as I got out a spoon and pulled the lid back on the yogurt. Dad opened the newspaper and began to read, his demeanor changing as he did. His shoulders relaxed as his eyes skimmed the articles. He picked up his mug and took a sip of his coffee.

I reveled in the familiarity of my father's body language as I finished my breakfast and then threw the container into the garbage. "If you're okay here, I'm going to head into the bathroom for a quick shower." I pointed to my stringy hair for emphasis.

Dad waved his hand in my direction. "I'm fine," he growled.

I nodded as I made my way down the hall and into the bathroom. I shut the door and turned on the water.

As steam filled the room, I felt my body relax. I pulled my hair from its bun and allowed it to fall down to the middle of my back.

I was going to take this time to relax, and then I'd face the day. And from what I'd already seen of it, it was going to be a long one.

By mid-morning, I was completely distracted with getting things ready to open the store. After my shower, I spent the morning doing paperwork amidst throwing in loads of laundry.

Dad stayed up until about nine and then fell asleep on the couch, watching the news. I tried to wake him to get him to go lie down in bed, but he wasn't having it. Instead, he tipped his head back and released a deep snore.

So I left him on the couch and went down to open the doors at nine forty-five on the dot.

Spencer was waiting outside with his hands shoved deep into his pockets. His shoulders were drawn up, and he was glancing around. He had a hat pulled down over his greying hair, and his beard had gotten longer. I shot him an apologetic smile as I unlocked the bolt and cracked the front door to the store.

"Sorry about that," I said.

He grunted as he waited for me to fully open the door, and then he barreled inside.

Spencer was an expert at fixing engines and just about anything that broke on the island, but he was not a people person. Dad snagged him twenty years ago while he was driving through town. Spencer had once worked in a pit crew for an undisclosed NASCAR driver and was fired— for an also undisclosed reason.

He was a little rough around the edges, but he was loyal to our family. I'd probably classify him as Dad's best friend. He was twenty years older than me and sort of an uncle figure in my life.

I just smiled as he shot over to his counter, flipped on the light, and disappeared into the back, where he kept all the machines that had been dropped off.

Feeling alone again, I turned the sign to open and glanced out the door. Downtown Magnolia was quiet for now. All the little shops that lined Main Street were just beginning to open.

Mrs. Crenshaw, who owned the antique shop across the street, was in the process of unlocking her door when she looked up. I waved at her only to have her deepen her scowl and disappear into her store.

I winced. I may have shaved Mrs. Crenshaw's cat when I was in middle school. And from her perpetual coolness toward me, Mrs. Crenshaw had never really forgiven me.

It didn't matter that I would never do something like

that now. After all, I was a responsible person who'd grown up to be a well-respected adult.

But that was the curse of living in the same small town where I'd grown up. Everyone still saw me as a pig-tailed little terror.

And that was never going to change.

3

MAGGIE

The silence was deafening as I sat in my mother's office two days later, clutching to my chest the proposal Bri helped me put together. My mind was reeling as I ran through my pitch for what felt like the millionth time since I let Bri talk me into this colossal mistake.

I should have told her no and put my foot down. I should have realized that, as soon as I walked into Penny's office, my entire body would shut down. I should have known it was best to leave my mother out of this.

But apparently, I was a glutton for punishment.

My breath caught in my throat, causing me to swallow hard. There was nothing about this situation that could make me feel better. Going to my mother with a proposal for her to help me with all of my problems? Was I an idiot?

I should have gone to my dad. He would have been

nurturing. He would have taken me under his wing and helped me come up with solutions. He would have offered to give me his entire retirement to save me from the mess I'd made. Which was why I couldn't go to him. He was barely making ends meet in Minnesota. I couldn't ask him to give me what he didn't have.

And Penny? Well, she had money in spades—and even more.

I always felt awkward around my own mother. Penny valued presentation. That was probably why she was one of New York's renowned editors. Every book she worked on went on to be an international best seller.

Penny knew how to take a book and clean it up until it sparkled.

It's too bad she didn't know how to do that with me.

Where Penny was elegant and graceful, I was average and clumsy. Penny had long legs, and me? I'd inherited Dad's short ones that resembled elephant stumps.

I always secretly wondered if Penny would request a maternity test. I knew she couldn't believe that such a klutzy, blonde-haired woman did in fact spring from her loins.

The sound of Penny's assistant typing on her computer made me glance up. Harper was sitting at her desk, with her bleached white hair and perky smile. She was young—twenty-something—and beautiful. I'd made the mistake of looking her up on social media only to find photos of her on business trips with Penny.

Here I sat, practically sweating through my suit coat,

waiting to speak to the woman who gave birth to me, yet the girl ten feet away from me had a better relationship with her than I did. It was hard not to feel like Penny had chosen a new daughter over me.

That was exactly what I *didn't* need right now. Another person in my life reminding me just how ridiculous I was. And how easy it was for people to ignore me.

Feeling self-conscious, I pulled at the hem of my pencil skirt in an effort to cover my thighs. Suddenly, my choice of outfit filled me with regret.

A pinstriped skirt with a dark-grey suit coat? What was I thinking? I should just claim stomach issues and run out of here. It would be less embarrassing than facing the beast with pit stains.

I had nothing good to tell Penny. She didn't know that Sean and I had split. She didn't know about my current unemployment. And my string of failed diet attempts was about as apparent as the nose on my face.

This entire idea was a mistake. It would be better if I called it quits now, while I still had a tiny shred of self-respect.

Just when I was about to stand and sprint out of the office, Harper's phone rang. The sound was shrill and grated on my nerves. My heart leapt in my chest as I waited for Harper to speak.

"Yes?" she asked in a syrupy sweet voice. Then her gaze snapped over to me, and heat instantly crept up my cheeks.

I fiddled with the hem of my jacket and then smoothed

down my skirt, hoping Harper couldn't see how rattled I was. My confidence could only go so low.

"Ms. Brown will see you now," Harper said as she set the phone back onto the receiver.

I tried not to snort as I gathered my purse and papers. "My *mother* will see me now?" I asked as I attempted a graceful walk in front of Harper.

From the corner of my eye, I saw her wrinkle her nose as I passed by. I had to admit, I felt the same. Saying *mother* like that felt as strange to hear as it did to say.

Before I could unpack those feelings, I found myself standing in front of Penny's office, staring at the dark mahogany door. I took in a deep breath as I raised my hand and knocked three times.

When no one answered, I did it again.

"If she phoned to tell you to come in, you just go in," Harper said from behind me.

I nodded quickly and moved my focus to finding the door handle while keeping all of my belongings in my arms. I fumbled to turn the handle. I had to lean against the door to open it, and I felt a sense of triumph when it finally began to move.

The door swung open before I anticipated it, causing me to stumble into the room. My papers and purse flew into the air and scattered across the floor in that sort of slow-motion effect you only see in the movies.

"Margaret." Penny's voice was sharp and annoyed.

I glanced up to see her standing over me with a disappointed expression etched on her not-surprisingly wrinkle-free face.

"Hi, Penny," I said as I scrambled to pick up my proposal. This meeting was off to a *great* start.

I could feel her disappointed stare, but I forced myself to focus on scooping my keys, wallet, and lip gloss back into my purse.

Once my belongings were where they should be, I smoothed down my skirt only to find that Penny had returned to her desk, which was situated in front of the floor-to-ceiling windows.

Feeling completely out of place, I cleared my throat and started to approach her. It had been a few months since we last spoke. Should I start with what I've been up to? My failed job search? My even more pathetic dating life?

How did I say anything without sounding completely incompetent?

I must have looked like a mess, because as soon as Penny raised her gaze to meet mine, her eyebrows went up and her lips parted. She pulled off her signature red glasses that she had perched on her nose. She took her time folding them and then set them on her desk in front of her.

"Stop gaping like a fish and sit, Margaret," she said, marking her words with an exasperated sigh.

I snapped my lips shut and swallowed, the embarrassment inside of me reaching an all-time high. If I were a cartoon, I would be a melted pile of goo on the floor by now.

Realizing that the longer I stood there, the greater chance I had of making another blunder, I crossed the room and collapsed onto the armchair across from Penny's desk. I set my stack of papers—which were a jumbled mess by now—on the side table next to me.

I attempted to cross my legs, but when Penny's gaze flicked down to my knees, I settled on sitting with my feet on the floor and my hands resting on my thighs.

Penny didn't speak as she pulled the chair away from her desk and sat down. Her back was straight as she set her hands on her desk. Her fingers were entwined, and she oozed propriety.

Heck, I wasn't going to wait for Penny to instigate a maternity test, I should just call it in myself. That this woman and I could possess the same DNA shocked me.

"I'm a busy woman, Margaret, so it's best if you just get to the point."

I laughed loudly, and it sounded a little shrill. Then I pinched my lips together as I nodded. "Right. Right."

Stop saying right.

I cleared my throat as I grabbed the pile of papers. I tapped the bottom of them onto my thighs and then stood, leaning across Penny's desk, to set them in front of her.

"I have a business proposition for you," I squeaked out as I settled back into the chair. After an awkward attempt at trying to figure out what to do with my hands—which I was pretty sure made me look like I was dancing like an Egyptian—I settled on resting them on my knees and glanced up at Penny, waiting for her to respond.

The silence that surrounded us felt as deafening as a scream. I swallowed hard, hoping the deodorant I'd put on earlier would be able to withstand the test my body was going to put it through.

Penny sighed as she rested her hands on the pile of papers. Then she glanced over at me, and all I wanted to do was crawl under the desk and hide.

There wasn't anger or frustration in Penny's gaze. All I saw was...pity.

And right now, I wasn't sure if that was worse.

"Why don't you just tell me your plan and we'll go from there," Penny said.

I stared at her, not quite sure what to do. It was as if all my preparation and hard work had been thrown out the window. Then I told myself to put on my big-girl panties and speak. This wasn't going to break me.

"I want to start my own interior design company. You know I graduated with honors from NYU. I've worked with some of New York's elite. It would be perfect, working for myself." My stream of thoughts erupted out of me before I could settle on a more dignified way of saying it.

Penny's eyebrows were raised as she studied me. "You want to start an interior design company?"

I nodded, thankful she was able to process what I'd said even if I couldn't.

Penny unfolded her hands and pointed a finger down on her desk as if she were making a clarification. "Here. In New York."

My confidence was waning. This was a stupid idea. Sean thought it was ridiculous, and now, so did Penny. "Yes," I said, my voice coming out as small as my confidence.

Penny studied me for a moment before she pushed her chair away from her desk and stood. Then she wandered over to the windows, where she rested her shoulder against the metal casing. I watched her, not quite sure what she was doing. Was this meeting over? Was this her way of telling me she was done listening?

"I know things haven't been the best between us..." Penny started but then allowed her words to trail off.

I glanced around, not sure if I was supposed to respond, so I settled on, "I know."

Penny glanced over her shoulder and met my gaze. She walked across the room, over to the side of her desk nearest me, and leaned against the edge so she could extend her feet in front of her.

"I want to help, but I can't just hand you the money."

"You wouldn't," I said, a bit too quick. Penny raised her eyebrows, and I felt like I was being reprimanded. It was subtle but effective. "Sorry," I whispered.

Penny folded her arms and tapped her fingers on her bicep. She alternated between studying me and dropping her gaze to the floor.

Worried that I was going to lose my one chance with

Penny, I straightened and forced my most businesslike demeanor. "It will be strictly a loan. I will pay it back, with interest. I know I shouldn't be asking you this. I'm sure you think it will be a joke, but I have to try. I'm...at a crossroads." My emotions bubbled up inside of me, causing me to blink a few times. I was sick of crying, and doing it in front of Penny wasn't an option.

Crying didn't speak to a confident, prepared business-woman. It said emotional and chaotic, and even if that was how I felt, I didn't need to confirm it to her. So I forced a smile.

Penny studied me for a moment, and right before I felt as if I were going to slip into insanity from the intensity one woman's stare could bring, Penny pushed off her desk. She walked gracefully over to the other side of the desk and sat down on her chair.

She pulled it forward just enough so she could rest her hands on top of the desk. "There's a house—in Rhode Island—that I've been holding onto for some time. Ever since your grandmother passed away five years ago."

I blinked. There was so much to unpack in that state-ment. "I had a grandmother that passed away?" Why was this the first time I was hearing this?

Penny waved away my words. "I told you. Besides, your grandmother and I hadn't spoken in years. Dorthy kept to herself." Penny raised her fingers to her temples and began to rub them. "That island was her world, and when she couldn't take care of the house, she moved to

California, where she stayed with her sister before she passed away."

So distancing oneself from one's daughter ran in this family. Good to know.

"I'm sorry," I said, and I meant it. It wasn't easy to live with the weight of a bad relationship hanging around your neck. To have that person die before you could reconcile had to hurt.

Penny's expression morphed to one of sadness for a moment before it flashed back. She shrugged. "What's done is done. Now, this house is run-down. It needs work. But it seems like the perfect task for an up-and-coming interior design company." Penny leaned back in her chair and bounced a few times.

I raised my eyebrows, waiting for the punchline. Was she serious? "Me? You want me to fix it up?" Was this a job or a test? I wasn't sure how to take it.

Penny steepled her fingers as she rested her elbows on the armrests of her chair. She tapped her forefinger on her lips as she stared at me. "It's a proposition. If you fix it up and I can sell it, you can have a portion of the proceeds to invest in"—she leaned forward and studied the business proposal that I'd laid in front of her—"Studio Red." Penny paused and glanced up at me. "Are you firm on that name?"

Even though I should have been a tad offended at her passive-aggressive way of saying she hated the name, I didn't want to scare off any offer until I was sure what was going on.

I raised a finger and leaned in. "You're saying if I fix up this house in Rhode Island, I can have the money?" My ears were ringing as my own words finally reached them.

Penny sighed. "Yes. Unless you don't think you're up to the task—"

"I'm up to the task," I said quickly as I fought the urge to smile like the Cheshire cat. "I'll do it." Wanting to seal the deal, I stood quickly and reached across the table to shake hands. In my haste, I lost my balance, and I had to frantically grab for the desk to steady myself.

In the process, I knocked over an award of some sort and it went crashing to the ground. Heat coursed through me as I dropped down to pick it up—silently praising just about every god that it hadn't broken—and set it on the desk.

"I'm sorry," I muttered.

Penny was staring at me when I reluctantly returned my gaze to her. Her lips were parted as she ran her gaze up and down me.

"It's all right." Then she furrowed her brow. "Are you sure—"

"I'm sure." I straightened and smoothed down my suit coat. "I can do this. I won't let you down."

Penny seemed hesitant, but thankfully, she finally pushed her chair back and slid open one of her desk drawers. She fished around and then pulled a key from inside.

"The house is on an island called Magnolia. Right across from Newport, Rhode Island." She handed the key to me and then pulled a sticky note from the pile in front of her and wrote something. "I will call Tessa. She's the realtor on the island. She'll meet you at the house and give you the rundown—what you'll need to do to make sure that I can get top dollar for the house."

She extended the note out to me. I took it, pressing the sticky part into my hand. Excitement was bubbling up inside of me, and it was getting harder and harder to push it down.

"Tessa. Island. Magnolia. Got it," I said as I committed each detail to memory.

"I expect weekly emails about the progress of the restoration. If you fail to do so..." Penny clicked her tongue as she shrugged.

She didn't have to go on. I knew what she was saying. I took a deep breath and nodded. "I won't disappoint you," I said, and I meant it.

Penny was taking a chance on me, and I was going to exceed her expectations if it killed me.

"Well then, I look forward to seeing the finished product. And I will expect one. This is a house that I am ready to sell. I have no intention of holding onto it any longer."

I wanted to ask why but decided against it. After all, she didn't look as if she wanted to continue the conversation as she returned her glasses to her nose and turned to face her computer. After a few seconds ticked by, Penny glanced over at me. "I have work to do," she said.

Feeling like an idiot, I nodded. "Yes. Of course. I'm out of here," I said as I scrambled to pick up my purse. Then I turned as a flood of emotions rushed through me. "Thanks, Mom," I said slowly, the feeling of that word leaving an impression on my tongue.

She paused as she studied me and nodded. "Remember, emails every week."

I gave her one last smile and then bolted to the door. Once I was through the lobby and had boarded the elevator, I let out a cheer. One that included pumping my fists in the air and dancing.

I didn't care that Harper and the random UPS guy were staring at me. I didn't care that Penny most likely heard me and there was a chance that she would pull this deal altogether.

I was picking up my crumbling life and moving forward. I was getting the chance that I was so desperate for.

And nothing was going to take that away from me.

Watch out world, Maggie Brown was back. And this time, I was here to stay.

4

CLEMENTINE

The sun burst through the open doors of the hardware store and spilled onto the floor in front of the counter. I set down the book I'd been reading and stretched back on the barstool. My back cracked as I reveled in the feeling of release that my muscles needed.

It was almost eleven on a Friday, and the shop was surprisingly quiet. It had to be the warmer weather. People were wanting to enjoy the island instead of being cooped up in their homes.

If I were honest with myself, I wanted to be outside instead of watching the store.

Too bad that wasn't an option for me.

Ever.

I settled back in my seat and brought my feet up to rest on the shelf just below the counter. I hunched over my knees and opened my book back up. It didn't take long to get lost in the story again, and I didn't look up until I heard the bells of the front door jingle.

Glancing up, I saw Tessa wander in. Her almost-white hair was pulled up into a bun on the top of her head. She was worrying her lips as she swept her gaze around.

"Hey, Tessa," I said as I slipped my bookmark into my book and set it next to the register, where it was hidden from view. I stood and leaned my elbows on the counter. "What are you looking for?"

Tessa shot me a smile as she made her way over to me, all the while fishing something out of her purse. "Do you have a screwdriver that could work for my glasses? The screw keeps coming out, and I'm blind as a bat if I don't have them."

I nodded as I rounded the counter and motioned toward the back. "I should. Let's go see."

Tessa's heels clicked on the cement floor behind me as she followed. "I'm such a klutz, and I'm running so behind," she murmured.

I glanced over my shoulder and took in her rumpled state. She did seem more out of breath than normal. "Is it a new move-in?" I asked as I led her down the screwdriver aisle and hesitated in front of the ones we carried.

"Yes. Old Magnolia Inn."

I paused and turned to study Tessa. "Magnolia Inn?"

She pinched her lips and nodded. "Yes. Apparently, Dorthy's granddaughter is coming to fix the place up."

"Granddaughter?"

Tessa nodded again. "She's some interior designer

coming from New York. She's here to restore it to its former glory and then sell it." A wave of sadness washed over Tessa's expression as she finished her sentence.

Magnolia Inn had been a tourist attraction for over fifty years. One day, Dorthy closed its doors, and it sat unused and rotting ever since. Dorthy passed away five years ago, and no one had known what was going to happen to the house. Unfortunately, the beautiful building was deteriorating.

I focused my attention back on the screwdrivers in front of me and located the smallest one we had. "Will this work?" I asked as I handed it over to Tessa.

She took it from me and proceeded to attempt to repair her glasses as she stood next to me. It wasn't a perfect fit, but she was able to get the screw most of the way down.

She slipped her glasses on and turned to smile at me. "Thanks. It wouldn't look too good if I was tripping all over myself when I meet Margaret."

Margaret? Even her name sounded pretentious. "Her name is Margaret?" I asked as I returned the screwdriver to the hook. "Margaret from New York?"

I wasn't sure why, but the idea of some big-city elitist blowing into our small community made me angry. And maybe just a tad jealous. But I'd never admit that to Tessa.

"That's right." Tessa shouldered her purse and grinned over at me. "Well, I'm off. Wish me luck?"

I wasn't sure for what, but I couldn't see the harm in it. "Good luck," I called after Tessa's retreating frame.

As soon as the door jingled shut behind her, the shop fell quiet yet again. I swallowed as I wandered back to the front, settled back down on my seat, and pulled out my book.

But no matter what I did, my mind couldn't stop thinking about this new move-in. Which was ridiculous. Getting the inn back in commission meant yet another tourist attraction which meant more business.

Plus, she was going to need tools, and we were here to provide that. But I couldn't get the nagging feeling out of my mind that this wasn't as good as I was attempting to make it out to be.

"Did you eat a lemon?" Archer's voice piped up from behind me.

I startled and flung my feet to the ground as I turned to glower at him. "No," I shot in his direction.

His eyebrows went up as he tousled his damp hair. "Well, you look like you did. Who ticked you off today?" he asked as he wandered over to the counter and grabbed a caramel from the small glass jar by the register.

I swatted his hand away and shot him an annoyed look to which he just shrugged and unwrapped the candy.

"Tessa was here."

Archer snorted. "That crazy lady?" His jaw was working the caramel as he folded his arms and leaned back against the counter.

"She's not crazy," I replied as I shoved his shoulder.

"What are you talking about? Before she was a realtor, she was a third-grade teacher. Don't you remember?"

I rolled my eyes. Of course I remembered. Tessa was a teacher before she got Archer and his gang of punks. She'd been such a sweet lady—until Archer made it his mission to hide her glasses.

She became a realtor the next year.

"You were horrible to her," I said as I grabbed a rag and began to shuffle around the items behind the counter as I dusted. I was anxious, and I wasn't sure why. Having a job seemed like the best thing to do to help alleviate my anxiety.

Archer sighed, and I heard the metal cover of the jar clang again. I straightened and shot him an annoyed look. "Will you stop that?" I asked.

He shrugged as he unwrapped the second caramel and popped it in his mouth. "It's a perk, right?"

I returned the lid and slid the container to the back counter and away from him. He settled in, folding his arms and squinting toward the front of the store. I followed his gaze to see that he was looking at…nothing.

"You okay?" I asked as I shook out the rag and returned it to the cupboard under the register.

Archer didn't respond. Instead, he continued to stare off as if he had something on his mind he was chewing on. Ever since Elise died and Collette left, he had these moments. It made me wonder if his thoughts were returning to his painful past.

It made me ache for my brother.

"Magnolia Inn is getting a new occupant," I said,

desperate to get my brother's attention off of whatever spiral he was heading down.

Archer blinked a few times before he sucked in his breath and turned his focus over to me. "It is? Who would buy that dump?"

I shrugged. "Apparently some high society from New York. She's here to remodel the place and sell it."

Suddenly, an idea popped into my head, and I turned to focus on Archer. My smile slowly spread across my lips, which caused Archer to groan.

"What is that look for?" Then he shook his head. "No. Nope. Not going to do it." He turned and began to head toward the back of the store. I followed after him. I wasn't going to let him go until he at least heard me out.

"Come on, Arch," I said as I tugged on his arm so he would turn his focus back to me.

Archer paused and glanced down. I attempted a consolatory smile to which he groaned and raised his arm up to break my contact with him.

"Whenever you get an idea in that little brain of yours, my life gets infinitely worse," he said as he brought his hand to my forehead and flicked it gently.

I swatted his hand away. "But it would be good for you."

Archer stopped moving and studied me again. "What? Now I'm interested."

I wiggled my eyebrows as I glanced back and forth. "You should go offer your services to the new move-in," I said with my voice low.

Archer pulled back. "I should what?" His expression morphed into one of disgust.

I punched his shoulder. "Not like that, this is a family place."

"Then what services could you possibly be talking about?"

I avoided his gaze as I fiddled with the price tag of the leaf blower next to us. "You're handy, and I'm guessing she's going to need all the help she can get." I peeked up at him as I attempted to gauge his reaction.

Archer was working his jaw, his muscles flexing. He was a teeth grinder when he was a kid, and I could only imagine the stress he was under now. It's strange that when something traumatic happens, we have a tendency to return to a habit that made us feel safe when we were younger.

"Plus, it would get you out of here and out into the world again. You have no social life," I said as I faced him and folded my arms across my chest.

"I have a social life," he scoffed.

I narrowed my eyes. "Hanging out at the pub with Tom and his gang is not a social life."

Archer eyed me, and a moment later, he was wrapping his arms around me and lifting me up. "I have you," he sang out.

I screamed as I clawed at his arms. "Put me down," I yelped.

He laughed as he spun me around until I was sure I

was going to vomit. Then he put me down and patted my head.

"What about you?" he asked. "You have no friends and, the last time I checked, no life."

I swallowed at the effortless transition from me lecturing him to him tearing down my defenses. Not wanting to address my lack of any life at all, I busied myself with organizing the shelf in front of me.

"I have a life," I said.

"Mm-hmm."

I glowered at him. "I have a business to run. I'm a workaholic." I shrugged like that was an obvious answer, so why did I even need to say it.

The smirk on his lips just made me angrier. I faced him as heat permeated my cheeks. "Someone has to be here for Dad."

Archer's smile left his lips as he studied me. Then he sighed as he pushed his hand through his hair and backed away. Our conversation had quickly morphed from one of teasing to something more serious. Something deeper.

Cue his hasty retreat. Right on time.

"I should go," he mumbled as he turned and made a beeline for the front door.

Tears pricked my lids. Anytime something serious came up, Archer left. I knew being around Dad was painful for my brother, but did he have to abandon me like this?

It wasn't fair.

Why did fate hate us like she did?

I headed over to Spencer's counter. I tapped my fingers on the glass top, and Spencer appeared. He had parts in each hand, and he looked annoyed that he was being bothered. I ignored his narrowed eyes.

"Can you hold down the fort while I check on Dad?" All it took was a mention of Dad, and his expression softened.

"Yeah," he mumbled as he set down the pieces in his hand and rounded the counter, taking off his oil-stained apron as he did. I gave him a quick nod as I hurried past him and over to the back door that led to the upstairs apartment.

When I entered, the place was quiet. I checked every room until I found Dad lying on his bed, books scattered around him. His mouth was open, and he was snoring loudly.

I smiled as I walked into the room and located a blanket. I gently laid it over him and then gathered up all the books and stacked them back on the nightstand next to him.

I drew the drapes closed slightly so the sun was no longer streaming onto his face. Then I tiptoed out and past the pictures that hung on the wall. Just as I cleared them, one caught my eye.

I paused and then turned to study it.

It was twenty summers ago. Dad had taken Archer and me fishing, and we'd caught the biggest fish that summer. I was standing next to Archer with a fish in my hand, and

Archer had one in his. The smiles on our faces were genuine. Natural.

My heart ached as I reached out and ran my fingers across the glass. Tears filled my eyes as I thought back to a time when I wasn't worried about the store or Dad or how much longer I had with him.

Archer was back, but for how long? How long until he spiraled again? He seemed put together, but all it took was one shake, and he would be gone. Again.

I was barely holding it together, and I wasn't sure how I would handle being alone.

If Dad left and Archer disappeared, who would I have?

No one. I'd have no one.

A tear slid down my cheek, and I angrily wiped it away. I hated it when I allowed myself to think this way. No one ever fixed their issues by moping about them. If I wanted to change my circumstances, it started with me. I could affect my future if I tried hard enough.

I was willing to try. After all, what did I have to lose?

Nothing but the potential of an already determined crappy future.

I was more than willing to give that up.

5

MAGGIE

The smell of salt blew around me on the moist ocean breeze as I stood in front of the enormous three-story house. I blinked a few times, trying to wrap my head around what I was staring at.

This wasn't the house. It couldn't be the house. This had to be a joke. A mean, oddly out-of-character joke for my mother.

There was no way that this was what she'd described.

The once-yellow paint was peeling and flaking. The shingles on the roof were curled and crumbling. Even from where I was standing, I could see the missing floorboards on the porch and broken windows on the second floor.

If Penny was trying to challenge me, this was the way to do it.

I blew out my breath as I stared down at the piece of

paper Penny had handed me. The handwriting was completely perfect and confirmed to me what I'd feared.

This was the place.

My test.

My new home away from home.

Great.

A strong breeze picked up, and suddenly, I was being whipped in the face by my hair. I sputtered and clawed it away from my eyes and lips.

It was almost as if Mother Earth knew that I was out of my league. I couldn't help but feel as if the wind was a sign that I should just pack up now and leave.

Doubt settled in my mind as I pulled out my phone from my purse and swiped it on. Maybe I should text Brielle. She always knew what to say to help me feel better. And right now, I wanted to feel better.

Just as I began to type out a message, the sound of a car pulling into the parking lot next to me drew my attention. Intrigued, I abandoned my text and shoved my phone back into my purse and straightened, shielding my eyes with my hand.

A woman who looked to be in her mid-fifties stepped out of the car. She adjusted her glasses as she glanced around, and as soon as her gaze landed on me, she lifted her hand and wiggled her fingers as she let out a little, "Yoo-hoo."

I don't know why, but I was suddenly put at ease. Maybe it was the friendly way she looked at me or the fact that she embodied the quintessential small-town resident. But whatever it was, it made me feel better.

Like I hadn't just made the biggest mistake of my life.

Clutching her purse to her stomach, the woman rushed up to me and pulled me into a hug. She smelled like lilacs and bleach, and her white hair tickled my nose. Not sure what to do, I reached my arm around and patted her on the back.

The woman pulled away and ran her gaze over me. "Margaret?" she asked.

I nodded. "Maggie actually."

The woman stepped back and extended her hand. "Tessa. Your mom told me you were coming. I'm so sorry I'm late."

I shrugged as I shook her hand. "I just got here, so you're right on time."

Tessa chuckled as she fished around in her purse and removed a key. "I like the way you think."

I followed after her as she walked across the parking lot and up the large, open staircase that led to the wraparound porch. The white paint on the wood was just as worn as on the siding, and I couldn't help but wince at the thought of how much it was going to cost to replace all the boards.

I definitely had my work cut out for me, that was for sure.

Penny had agreed to provide a stipend, and I was rapidly seeing those numbers decrease the more I studied this house.

Tessa didn't seem to notice my distracted manner. Instead, she was rambling on about the history of the house. How long it had stood for and the numbers of owners it had before me. Apparently, it was called Magnolia Inn and was an institution here on the island.

She unlocked the front door and handed the keys over to me as she ushered me inside.

The air was stuffy, which was a stark contrast to the salty breeze outside. I took a moment to smooth down my hair as I glanced around.

The hardwood floors were scraped and worn. The walls were covered with floral wallpaper. But there was a certain charm to the details in the crown molding and wood accents that got my heart pounding.

I walked over to the large staircase that hugged the side of the wall. I ran my fingers across the wood banister, leaving a trail in the dust. I sucked in my breath as excitement stirred in my stomach.

Sure, fate seemed to have it out for me. Every step I'd taken in the past felt wrong, but none of them had me as excited as standing in this rundown house did.

It felt as if this was the place I was meant to be.

"I take it you like it," Tessa's voice pulled me from my thoughts as she approached.

I glanced over at her to see her wide smile as she stared at me. I cleared my throat and nodded. "It feels like this is the right place for me," I said as I moved over to the large wood check-in desk next to the stairs. There were scattered papers across the desk, and I picked one up. It was an ad for some diner in town.

"Ah, Magnolia Eatery. You'll have to try it out. The food there is delicious," Tessa said as she pointed her finger to the image on the sheet.

I nodded and set the paper back down. Then I took one more glance around the foyer before looking back at Tessa, who was watching me. I gave her a quick smile and then shrugged.

Thankfully, she could pick up on hints. I was ready to bring my stuff in and spend some time alone, exploring. Tessa was nice, but I wasn't sure I had much more to say to her.

"I'll head out," she said as she gave me a quick smile and made her way to the front door. "Make sure to stop by after you get settled in. I can show you all the fun places to go in Magnolia and introduce you to the people." She stopped with her hand on the door handle and nodded. "You'll like it here. It's not New York, but it's a small town with great people. They are all excited to see Magnolia Inn restored to its former glory."

I gave her a soft smile and a nod. Nothing like piling on the pressure. Not only did I have Penny depending on me, but now an entire town. What if I failed?

With my history, it was pretty evident that I was going to fail. It was my destiny. The thought that I just might disappoint all of these people broke me inside.

I let out a nervous chuckle as I shrugged. "I guess I'll have to work hard, then," I said.

Tessa grinned as she pulled open the door. "I have no doubt that you'll be great." She gave me one last reassuring smile and slipped outside, shutting the door behind her.

I blew out my breath as I surveyed the house. Thankfully, it didn't look as bad on the inside as it did on the outside. Despite the outdated fixings, I could tell the bones were good. That thought got my heart pumping.

I was going to be cautiously optimistic. If I let myself get too excited, I would have that much farther to fall when things didn't turn out like I wanted them to. I'd learned to keep my expectations low, so I'd never be disappointed.

Heat crept up my skin, so I reached up and gathered my hair into a bun at the top of my head. After securing it, I took the stairs two at a time to the second story. After a quick look around, I noted the state of each room. There were eighteen in all. Five along the farthest wall, as well as four on the other. The same for the third floor.

On the main floor were the owner's quarters—aka, my room—the kitchen, dining room, living room, and the outside door that led to a patio with a gazebo covering most of it.

I rested my hands on my hips as I surveyed the owner's room. I couldn't help the smile that twitched on my lips. The room was the size of my old apartment. There was a small bathroom with a claw-foot tub and a pedestal sink that had to be original to the house.

A tiny medicine cabinet hung above the sink, and

despite the fact that the glass was cloudy, I was going to keep it. How could I not? I loved the age the mirror gave off, and I couldn't help but think of all the people in the past who'd stood in front of it.

Did my grandmother stand here? For a moment, I allowed my thoughts to wander to her. Did I look like her? Why hadn't Penny ever talked about her before?

It was strange, but the desire to get to know her rose up inside of me. I was ready for a positive mother-figure in my life, and my grandmother just might serve that role.

I reached out and twisted the sink's cold faucet handle, and the pipes groaned. It took a few seconds, but finally water came out. Well, water was a joke. The yellowish-brown substance that poured from the faucet smelled like death.

I wrinkled my nose as I hurriedly turned off the water and sighed. I was going to need to find a plumber right away. I wasn't sure how effective bathing in the ocean would be, and I wanted to make a good impression with the residents of Magnolia. My stringy hair and smelly body wasn't the way to do that.

Despite the status of the water in the inn, I wasn't going to let that bring me down. Instead, I smoothed down my shirt as I walked out of the bathroom. I was going to bring in my sparse belongings and get situated. Then I'd venture into town.

The temperature had cooled slightly as I left the inn. I took in a deep breath, reveling in the feeling of the fresh air in my lungs. It was such a stark difference from the muggy, smelly New York atmosphere.

Just as I reached the trunk of my car, my phone rang.

I startled and hurried to pull it from my back pocket. It was Brielle.

I couldn't fight the smile as I pressed the talk button and brought my phone up to my ear.

"Hey," I said as I pulled open the trunk and grabbed one of the many overflowing laundry baskets I'd stacked in there like Jenga.

"Did you get there? Are you safe? Have you been kidnapped by a trucker at a rest stop?" she asked, not pausing to take a breath.

Laughing, I rested the basket on my hips and pinned the phone between my cheek and my shoulder as I reached in to grab another basket.

"I'm fine. I just got here about an hour ago," I said. I turned and headed back into the inn, where I set the baskets down in my room. There was no bed, but thankfully, I'd had enough forethought to order one with the few remaining dollars I had in my bank account.

The bed was coming tomorrow, so I was going to have to survive sleeping on the wood floor until then. Which I was okay with.

I pushed the loose strands of hair from my face and headed back out to the car.

"Well, I miss you. Who am I going to hang out with now?" Brielle whined.

I smiled as I reached in to grab a suitcase and a pillow-case full of items from my trunk. "Brielle, you have Brent and way more friends than I do. I think you'll be fine."

Just as I straightened, the bright smile and tousled brown hair of a woman who'd suddenly appeared in front of me caused me to scream.

The phone slipped from my shoulder, and the bags dropped to the ground.

"Oh my gosh, I'm so sorry," the woman said as she hurried to pick up the phone and hand it over to me.

My hands shook as I nodded and retrieved the phone from her grasp. Brielle was freaking out—I could hear her panic before I even brought the phone back to my ear.

"What's going on?" she asked, her voice full of desperation.

"I've gotta go," I said.

"Wait, are you okay?"

I nodded but then felt stupid because Brielle couldn't see me. "Totally fine." I spoke quickly and hung up the phone before she could reply. By the time I slipped my phone back into my pocket, my nerves had calmed.

I felt like I could breathe again.

"Never sneak up on a New Yorker," I said. "People who do get stabbed." I gave her a smile just to let her know that I wasn't a crazy person. Which I was beginning to doubt.

The woman had bent down to retrieve the suitcase and pillowcase I'd dropped. When she straightened, she shot me an apologetic shrug.

"Sorry," she said. "I'll keep that in mind for the future." Then she turned and began to make her way across the parking lot and over to the front door.

Not sure what she was doing—could she be helping me? why?—I hurried to grab a few more items from the trunk and followed after her. When we got inside, I led her to the back, where my room was.

"Name's Maggie," I said as I set the items down next to each other.

"Clementine," she said. Upon closer inspection, I realized she looked about my age. I know it was a completely preschool reaction, but butterflies erupted in my stomach.

Could we be friends? I hoped so.

"Nice to meet you," I said as I wiped my sweating hands on my pants and then extended one.

She shook it. "So, New York, huh?" she asked.

I sighed. "Yep. My life was…" I let my statement trail off as I eyed her. How much of my life did she want to know? I wanted to be open and honest, but I also didn't want to reveal how much of a loser I was all in one go. I kind of wanted that to unfurl over time rather than hit her over the head with it.

But when her eyebrows rose, I knew she was waiting for me to continue.

"My life was in shambles," I said. "I needed a change of scenery."

Clementine smiled. "So you came to Magnolia to do that?"

We fell into step with each other as we made our way back out to my car.

I shrugged. "There really wasn't much for me back in New York." I grabbed a few items, and Clementine did as well.

"There's not a lot here in Magnolia," she whispered. I had to lean in to hear her words, she'd dropped her voice so low.

I eyed her as we walked back into the inn. "Been here a long time?"

She sighed. "My whole life. I run the hardware store here."

"Really? That's awesome. With the state of this place, I'll definitely be visiting your store."

Clementine laughed. "That's good."

We finished unloading my trunk and lingered in my room. I liked having Clementine around. It beat being in this huge house alone. I started laying out my comforter on the floor along with a pillow. Clementine picked up my light and then stood there as if waiting for me to direct her where to put it. Her gaze swept the room. "Are you staying here tonight? On that?"

I set my stuff down and then stood, brushing off my hands. "Yeah. Nowhere else to go."

"You don't have a bed"—she stepped into the hallway and then back into the room—"or any furniture."

I shrugged. "It's okay. I'll survive. I think my mattress-in-a-box gets delivered tomorrow. I can spend a night on the ground. It'll be like I'm camping." I gave her a wide smile, but she didn't look impressed.

"That's it. I would be a terrible Magnolia resident if I didn't offer you my couch." She tapped her chin with her finger. "Now, you may have to fight Archer for it, but I'm pretty sure you can take him." Her voice trailed off as she focused her attention on me. "It actually might be a good thing for you two to meet."

I pressed my hand to my chest. "Me? Why?" I really hoped she wasn't the *you're single and I have a single brother* type of person. I was nowhere near ready to date.

Ever.

"He needs work. Right now, he thinks occupying my couch is his job."

Great. She was that kind of person. The *I can't motivate my brother so maybe you could type.* I didn't need a project. I was having a hard enough time with myself and this inn.

"I'm…" How could I put this delicately? I'd just met her and was enjoying the potential friendship. I didn't want to scare her away.

She turned her attention to me and quickly waved her hand in front of her face. "Look at me. I'm so sorry. I just met you and already I'm overwhelming you." She grabbed my hand and practically pulled me from the room. "Let's go get some dinner, and we can talk about it there," she said over her shoulder.

Not wanting to say no, and becoming very aware of the grumbling in my stomach, I didn't fight Clementine. Instead, I grabbed my packed overnight bag—left over from my drive to Magnolia—and let her drag me all the way to her car.

I could finish unpacking my room tomorrow. For now, I was ready to relax and enjoy my new life, because it looked like it was going to be heads above where I had been.

And that thought excited me.

6

CLEMENTINE

I t wasn't until I had Maggie in my car that I realized how serial-killer I must have seemed. I'll admit, I was a little excited to find that the new move-in wasn't some big-city snob. Instead she was a regular joe like me. It was refreshing, and I may have gotten a little carried away.

Mom always told me I acted before I thought, and sitting next to Maggie in my car as we drove down Magnolia Drive was proof of that. Thankfully, Maggie seemed like a go-with-the-flow kind of person and had obliged my stalkerish actions.

As I slowed at the stoplight, I glanced over and gave her a sheepish smile. "I'm not crazy, I swear," I offered and then winced. People who were crazy always said that they weren't crazy. It didn't make their statement any truer.

Maggie glanced over at me and then shrugged. "You remind me of Brielle, which is a good thing."

I nodded as the light changed to green, and I pressed on the gas. "Brielle? Is she your friend in New York?"

I saw Maggie nod from the corner of my eye.

"Yep. She's my best friend." There was reverence in her voice that caused me to pause. She sounded as if she were deep in a memory, and I didn't want to interrupt that.

"Well, I'm honored, then," I said as I flicked on my blinker and took a left. I was going to take her to Shakes, the best hamburger joint on the island. My stomach growled in anticipation.

"So what does one do on the island?" Maggie's question threw me off balance, and for a moment, I wasn't sure what to say.

"What do *I* do on the island? Or what does *one* do on the island? Those are two different things entirely."

She chuckled. "What do *you* do?"

That was a loaded question even if it was simple. "Well, I work and…that's about it." I pulled into the parking lot and turned off the engine.

"And they say New York is the city that never sleeps." She twisted in her seat until she was facing me. "You're telling me there's nothing you do for fun here?"

I laughed out loud. Fun. That was a word I hadn't heard in a long time. I must have startled her, because she pulled back and raised her eyebrows. I held up my hand, feeling bad for my outburst. "I'm so sorry. I'm not laughing at you. It's just…" I sighed as I turned my gaze out of the car.

Maggie raised her hand. "I'm so sorry. I overstepped. If you don't want to tell me, that's fine."

Feeling like an incompetent dork, I shook my head. Why was I reacting like this? It was a simple question, and yet I couldn't seem to say anything.

"I dance," I whispered. My chest clenched as the words left my lips. I hadn't said that sentence in a long time. I should have added *used to*, but I couldn't bring myself to say it. Maybe it was because, perhaps someday, my words might actually be true.

And I wanted them to be true.

"You do? What kind?"

I pulled my keys from the ignition and pulled on the door handle. Maggie did the same, and soon, we were walking toward the entrance of the restaurant. Our shoes crunched on the gravel under our feet.

I shrugged as I pulled open the door and held it for her. "Everything? Mostly hip-hop, though it has been so long, I'm sure I'm completely out of the loop on what is popular anymore."

"You are? Why?" she asked as Brenda, the owner of Shakes, grabbed two menus and waved us over to an empty booth. It was the start of the tourist season in Magnolia, and the tables had begun to fill with all sorts of vacationers.

I thought about that as I slipped into the booth. I ordered a strawberry milkshake, and Maggie ordered a chocolate one. We paused our conversation for a moment as we read over the menu, and when Brenda returned, we both ordered the same thing—a cheeseburger with fries. Brenda nodded, took our menus, and hurried off.

I sighed as I entwined my fingers together and set them on the table in front of me. "Can I say *life?*"

Maggie glanced up at me as she sipped on her shake. "For what?" she finally asked.

"For your question earlier."

She furrowed her brow, and then recognition passed over her face as she nodded. "Right. For why you're out of touch." She stirred her straw in her shake as a thoughtful expression passed over her face. "So why don't you try again?"

I picked bits off of the straw wrapper in front of me. It was nice for someone to finally ask me questions about myself. For so long, my life had revolved around Archer and Dad. I was beginning to feel like I didn't have a voice or an opinion that anyone cared about.

"Time?" I offered. And that was true. Taking care of Dad was okay now, but things were only going to get worse. I needed to be ready for the day when he wasn't going to be able to be left alone for any period of time. And then what was I going to do?

She sighed. "I get that. I just got out of a horrible relationship with a man who sucked away so much of my time that I began to forget who I was." Her expression stilled as she met my gaze. "But I realized I needed to stop living for others and start thinking about myself."

I swallowed as emotions rose up in my throat. I knew

what she was saying was true, but I didn't want to think of caring for my Dad as something I just needed to stop doing. Even if I knew the inevitable question of if I could take care of him or not loomed in the distance.

I wasn't ready to deal with it, and I was certainly not ready to process how I felt about a memory care home. Not wanting to be a downer, I gave her a broad smile and said, "You're right. I'll keep that in mind."

Our food was delivered, and we spent the rest of the meal eating and talking. I made sure to keep our conversation light so we didn't slip down into the serious depths we'd reached earlier.

I was already fighting with Archer about what to do with Dad, and I didn't need another person pushing me. I knew that Maggie meant well. I was just stubborn. I was going to take my time before I decided anything, and I wasn't going to be pressured.

Not that Maggie was pressuring me, it was just a tough subject, one that I didn't take lightly. It was better for me to ignore it than to face it at this moment.

Just as we paid the check, my phone chimed. Glancing down, I saw it was a text from Archer. He and Dad were hungry, and he was wondering when I was coming home.

I rolled my eyes as I stuffed my phone into my purse and shot Maggie an apologetic smile. "I'm so sorry. Do you mind waiting a few minutes while I have Brenda whip me up something to take home? Apparently my brother forgot how to make dinner."

Maggie laughed as she nodded. "Of course."

I put in the order with Brenda, and Maggie and I moved to the side to stay out of the way. She had been in the middle of telling me about interior design, and I was eager to return to that conversation. Just as she parted her lips to speak, Victoria's familiar voice filled the air, cutting Maggie off.

I turned and attempted not to roll my eyes. Victoria Hold. Magnolia's youngest mayor and gossip queen extraordinaire. Her red hair was pulled up into a tight bun at the top of her head, and she was wearing a pressed suit on a Friday. At night.

She was ridiculous.

Her eyebrows rose up, and I realized that she'd asked me a question. I sighed as I leaned in. "What did you say?"

Her lips pursed as she looked from me to Maggie and then back. "I said, aren't you going to introduce me to your friend?"

I glanced over at Maggie, who eyed me. Then she extended her hand. "Margaret Brown, but you can call me Maggie. I just moved into the Magnolia Inn."

Victoria widened her eyes as she shook Maggie's hand. "Right. Tessa informed me that you were coming. How have you been enjoying Magnolia?"

I sighed. Loudly, so that Victoria could hear. She'd graduated a year after me, and if it hadn't been for the fact that her dad was a state senator, she would have never been elected. Her head was definitely bigger than most doorways. "She only just got here."

"I only just got here," Maggie replied as she smiled. "I'll let you know once I get to know the town."

Victoria studied Maggie and then smiled. "Wonderful. Well, let me know if there's anything I can help with. It may be hard getting the approval from the city council for another inn to open up, but with me by your side…" She let her voice trial off as she pursed her lips as if that was the answer to all of life's problems.

I tried not to groan. "I think she'll be okay."

Victoria shot me an annoyed look but then returned to her fake political smile as she faced Maggie. "Just in case, I'm here," she said.

Maggie nodded. "I'll keep that in mind. Thanks."

Victoria smiled. "Wonderful."

Just as she parted her lips to speak, Brenda walked up with a plastic bag overflowing with Styrofoam boxes. I grabbed it from her and nodded toward the door. "We should get going. We've got people waiting," I said as I patted the bag.

Victoria didn't respond—not that I bothered waiting to hear if she had something to say—as we made our way out to the parking lot.

Once we were inside my car, we buckled our seatbelts, and I saw Maggie studying me. I shrugged and threw the car into reverse.

"Victoria and I grew up together," I offered as I pulled out onto Magnolia Drive and headed toward the hardware store.

Maggie chuckled. "I get it. I'm good at reading people,"

she said as she folded her arms. Then she grew silent. "I guess I should change that to: I know how to read women. Men? I stink at that."

My thoughts suddenly shifted to Jake Palmer, which took me aback for a moment. I'd worked so hard for so long to push him from my mind—and for him to return like that, well it took my breath away.

I swallowed as tears formed on my lids, and I blinked angrily as I tried to dispel them. He was gone. He left. He didn't deserve to occupy my thoughts. Not now. Not ever.

I forced a laugh as I turned into the hardware parking lot and made my way to the back. After I pulled into my parking spot, I glanced over at her. "I bet you're not that bad."

Maggie scoffed as she reached in the back and grabbed the small overnight bag she'd brought. "Someday, I'll tell you about Sean over a bottle of wine and a platter of cheese."

I retrieved Dad and Archer's food and slammed the door at the same time as Maggie. We walked next to each other as we made our way to the back door and up the back stairs. "I'm looking forward to it," I said.

Maggie waited as I unlocked the door and pushed inside. The sound of the news playing on the TV carried out into the hall, and I did a quick check to make sure my family was decent before I waved Maggie in.

Dad was sitting on the couch with his eyes closed, and Archer was next to him, fiddling on his phone. He had on a t-shirt and jeans—which was a surprise. I half expected him to be walking around in his boxers.

"Food," I exclaimed.

Archer jumped from the couch. "Finally," he growled as he whipped around. Then he stopped in his tracks, his gaze roaming over Maggie and then over to me. "Who's this?" he asked.

I set the food down on the counter and motioned for Maggie to walk further into the apartment. "This is Maggie. She's the new owner of Magnolia Inn. She's going to stay with us for the night, so she's not sleeping on her floor." I pulled open the food bag and began setting out the containers. Once I found Dad's burger, I grabbed a plate.

Archer's shock must have worn off because a moment later, he was standing next to me. "Shouldn't you be checking with me before you bring people here to stay?" he asked in a mocking tone.

We'd had a very similar conversation about him and the little friends he wanted to have crash here when he first moved back to Magnolia.

I glared at him. The last thing I needed was for him to make Maggie uncomfortable. "She's a friend and my guest. I expect you to treat her as such." I threw the words over my shoulder as I made my way over to Dad and set his plate down on the side table next to him.

I reached out and wrapped my hands around his. "Hey, Dad," I said softly.

Dad grunted, and his eyes slowly opened. His gaze was

hazy at first, but then recognition passed through it as he studied me. "Janet?" he asked as he reached out and rested his weathered hand on my cheek.

My stomach plummeted as I fought the tears that threatened to spill. "No, it's Clementine. I brought you some food," I said, waving toward his dinner.

Dad look confused, but he followed my gesture and that seemed to distract him enough. Instead of entering into another round of who I was and who he was to me, he reached over and grabbed his plate and dove into his food.

I made my way back to the kitchen and to the awkward atmosphere that Archer had forced Maggie into. Instead of talking to her, he was leaning against the counter with his legs extended. He was shoveling food into his mouth like he hadn't eaten in weeks.

I grabbed a water bottle from the fridge and cracked it open. I needed to do CPR on my brother's social skills, and I needed to do it fast. If I was going to convince Maggie to take him on, I needed to show that he wasn't this socially inept person. I wanted to convince her that, yes, she did want to hire him.

After I dropped the water off with Dad, I made my way into the kitchen. Archer must have sensed my intention because his cheeks were swollen and his hamburger was almost gone. He was eating his food at a speed that I hadn't seen since he was on the football team in high school.

"So, Archer, you know that Maggie is restoring the inn," I started off.

Archer glared at me as he continued to chew. Fail number one for him—he'd shoved so much food into his mouth that he couldn't speak, allowing me to do all the talking.

Maggie laughed softly. "That's right," she offered.

Archer glanced over at her and gave her a weak smile. "That's nice," he said after he swallowed—wincing as he did it. Then he marched over to the fridge and grabbed out a water bottle.

"Which reminds me, do you guys know of a plumber on the island? My water is a color..." Her nose wrinkled. "It's a color I'm not sure how to describe."

"Archer," I exclaimed just as Archer said, "Patrick."

I narrowed my eyes. "Patrick is old. You don't want him." I hurried to interject.

Archer widened his eyes as he leaned in. "He'll do great," he said.

I shook my head, completely ignoring the hints of desperation that Archer was throwing my direction. Instead, I reached out and patted him on the back. "No one is as good at restoration projects as Archer is. There's nothing he can't do." I nodded toward him. "He's your man."

A silence fell around us, and I could feel my brother shooting daggers my direction. I offered him a wide smile, and I hoped the look in my eyes told him I wasn't backing down.

I liked Maggie, and there was no way I was saddling her with an eighty-something man who should have retired years ago. Not when Archer—who himself needed something to do other than be a thorn in my side—was perfectly capable.

And maybe I was hoping that if he saw he could actually be good at something, it might give him the confidence to start his life over again.

"Well, that would be great," Maggie said as she raised her hand. "I mean, if you're willing."

Archer cleared his throat and shot me one more annoyed look before he turned his attention toward Maggie. "I'd be happy to help," he said.

I smiled at Maggie, whose expression turned to one of relief.

"That's great. I was wondering how I was going to shower with no water."

Archer cleared his throat again as he grabbed his water bottle and tipped it toward Maggie. "I can start tomorrow."

Maggie nodded. "Perfect."

Archer glared at me as he walked past and down the hallway, where he shut his bedroom door.

I smiled at Maggie, who gave me an unsure smile back. "Are you sure this is okay? He doesn't seem too happy."

I shrugged as I grabbed out a bottle of water and offered it to her. "That's just the way his face is. He'll be fine. He needs this."

She thanked me as she took the water, and we made

our way over to the table and sat down. I wasn't sure if I should feel guilty that I was pushing my brother off on this newcomer. She was sweet, and Archer? Well, he could be like a grizzly on his bad days, but as gentle as a butterfly on his good days.

If I were honest with myself, I knew his bad days outnumbered his good ones, but that hadn't always been the case. A tiny bit of guilt crept up inside of my chest at that thought.

But I couldn't think like that. I had to believe that my brother still existed behind that hard exterior he was putting off. All he needed was someone or something to remind him that life was worth living.

If that meant working for Maggie, so be it.

I was ready to have my brother back. I was already losing my dad, I couldn't lose him as well.

Plus, Maggie needed help on the inn, so it was a win-win.

Right?

7

MAGGIE

I laid on Clementine's couch, staring up at the ceiling above me. Darkness surrounded me, and the only light that shone into the room was coming from the open window on the far end of the wall. I was pretty sure the anxiety of the move, mixed with the whiplash I felt from meeting Clementine, had my internal clock all out of whack.

I was having a hard time falling asleep, and from the jitters coursing through my body, I doubted I would ever be able to sleep again.

I groaned as I rolled to my side and picked up my phone from the coffee table. I pressed the side button and the screen lit up. I squinted at the sudden light, but that only lasted for a moment before my eyes adjusted.

12:30

Ugh. So much of the night left to go.

I knew that Clementine was trying to be nice by offering me a place to sleep, but I was regretting it. I had a feeling that after unpacking my car and settling in, I would have fallen asleep—snoring—on my makeshift bed.

But I was excited to have a friend here in Magnolia, and I really didn't want to reject her goodwill. So I lay there, trying to sleep but finding it impossible to do. Especially when my mind kept returning to Archer. He was brooding and mysterious and fine as…well, he looked like a movie star, I'll leave it at that.

I felt like a commoner standing next to him. And when he stared at me? I felt like my entire body was on fire. Thankfully, Clementine distracted me enough to keep me from saying something stupid to him. Archer had left shortly after he finished eating, which helped alleviate the stress I felt to be on my game.

Coming to Magnolia and falling for a guy was not on my list of things to do. Romance and I didn't mix. I needed to remember that. Especially when I looked into Archer's deep brown eyes or when his curly hair fell over his forehead and my fingers begged to swipe it away.

That would just make my friendship with Clementine that much more awkward, and that was not what I wanted. She seemed to dote on Archer as well as her dad. Who, from what I could tell, was struggling with something.

If I had to guess, it would be Alzheimer's, but I didn't want to outright ask Clementine. If she wanted me to know, she would tell me. I just had to wait and trust that she would eventually open up.

Fed up with trying to force sleep, I rolled to my back and opened my favorite Korean drama app. If I was going to be awake, I might as well drown my sleeplessness with some romance. Plus, reading subtitles might help my eyes grow tired, which in turn might help me finally fall asleep.

I could at least hope.

It didn't take long for me to engross myself in the show, and a short time later, I felt my eyelids grow heavy and I let them slip closed. My entire body relaxed, and I could feel myself drift into dreamland.

I suddenly felt the entire weight of what felt like a grizzly bear drop onto my body. "What the—" a gruff voice growled.

My eyes flung open, and I yelped as I tried to move my arms, legs, anything that would stop me from being crushed under the weight of whoever was sitting on me.

"Hey!" I said. But with a significant reduction in lung capacity, my voice came out a whisper. I pushed on the grizzly's back, but they didn't budge.

Finding the strength to fight, I shoved as hard as I could, and suddenly, the weight was lifted off my body. I watched as the shadow moved over to the side table, and suddenly, the room was bathed in light.

Archer was standing next to the table with his shoulders rounded. His eyebrows were knit together and he looked like he was about to attack. I could smell alcohol, and I was pretty sure it was coming from him. He'd either drunk himself into a stupor or he'd bathed in it.

"Archer?" I asked, hoping he'd realize that I knew him and he knew me. The last thing I needed was for him to think I'd broken in and...fallen asleep on his couch. Which, to a person not under the influence, made no sense. But Archer didn't look like he knew what the alphabet was much less how to string the letters together.

He stared at me as recognition slowly passed over his face. His expression softened, and suddenly he crossed the room and pulled me into a hug. I stood there, stunned. I couldn't move my arms—he was pinning them to my sides—and I couldn't step away.

Never in my life had I been hugged that hard by someone. Sean used to feel like a limp fish in my arms. Not Archer. He was holding onto me like I was a life raft and he was drowning.

When he buried his face into the crevices of my neck, my entire body pounded from the intensity that emanated from his touch. He was going through something, and I couldn't figure out if he realized it was me he was holding onto or someone else.

"I'm sorry," he whispered. His warm breath on my neck sent shivers across my skin.

Not wanting to just stand there as he hugged me like his life depended on it, I bent my elbow and patted his back. "For what?" I asked, softly.

He groaned, and I worried for a moment that I'd done the wrong thing.

"For Elise. I—" His voice broke, and he pulled back, staring down at me. I could see tears gather in his eyes as he held my gaze. "It was my fault. It was all my fault. I shouldn't have said those things to you." He reached up and cradled my cheek with his hand. It was warm and big, and it fit perfectly against my face.

"It's okay," I said. I wasn't sure what he'd done, but it couldn't be that bad that he'd drunk himself into a stupor over it. Whatever he did to Elise had to be forgivable. Whomever he thought I was had to have the capacity to forgive him. So if I could give him a tiny sense of peace, I would.

He blinked a few times as he stared down at me. It was almost as if he were suddenly coming to his senses. But that look passed, and he shifted to the side. He collapsed on the couch with his face buried in the armrest and his feet dangling off the other end.

I stood there, trying to figure out what I was going to do. Waking him didn't seem possible. If he could stand there and have an entire conversation with me and not know it was *me*, there was no way he was moving from his current spot.

I ran my gaze over his body and took note of his shoes that were still on his feet. I eyed them. Was it too weird for me to take them off?

Then, shaking that thought from my head, I reached down and gave them a hard tug. After a bit of work, I was able to pull them off, and I set them down over by the front door. When I returned to Archer, he hadn't moved an inch. So I found a nearby throw blanket and shook it out over him.

I folded my arms and ran my gaze around the room. Where was I supposed to go now? The armchair on the other side of the couch didn't look large enough to hold me. I wandered over to the room that I'd seen Archer disappear into earlier.

Was that his room? If it was, did that mean there was an empty bed?

Exhausted and ready to go to sleep, I forced my fears from my mind and pushed open the door. The room was small but tidy. There were a few pieces of clothing scattered on the floor, and it smelled like what I could only assume was his cologne—spice and musk—but it looked hospitable.

And his bed was made and currently empty. For me, that was good enough.

I quietly shut his door, walked across the room, and crawled into his bed. It must have been my exhaustion or the fact that I was emotionally spent from whatever Archer had dragged me into, but as soon as my head hit my pillow, I was out.

I didn't wake up again until the next morning when the sun poured through the open blinds right onto my face. I groaned as I pulled the comforter up over my head. There was no way I wanted to get up. It was the first day of the rest of my life, and call me crazy, but I wanted to sleep in.

Until realization dawned on me and I suddenly remembered where I was.

I was in Clementine's house...in her brother's bed.

I moved to throw off the covers, but just as I did, the door swung open. Scared that I was going to be caught, I pulled the covers back up over my head, my eyes peeking out from a small crack between the blanket and the bed.

My heart began to pound as I watched Archer walk into the room. His hair was damp, and it clung to his face. He had on just a towel, and I could see the remnant beads of water from his shower still clinging to his chest.

His incredibly toned chest.

I swallowed as he paused and his gaze fell on me. It seemed as if he were waiting to see if I was awake. I felt paralyzed on his bed as I waited for him to do whatever he was going to do and leave.

He must have figured that I was asleep because he walked over to his closet and began to rifle around inside of it. He pulled out a t-shirt and slipped it on. And then his towel dropped, and I clamped my eyes shut, heat permeating every inch of my body. I was pretty sure the entire bed would catch on fire.

Thankfully, it wasn't too long before I heard the sound of the door latch engaging. I cautiously opened my eyes and looked around. I breathed a sigh of relief as I flung the covers off and stared up at the ceiling above me.

That was...awkward. Weird. Strange.

I was pretty sure I was never going to be able to face

Archer again. Not after what happened last night and now this morning.

I might as well just throw in the towel on mine and Clementine's friendship. I wasn't sure I could come back from this.

Not wanting another Archer incident, I hurried to climb off his bed. I threw the comforter back on so it at least looked like I tried to make it. I was ready to get out of here and over to the inn.

Just as I pulled open the door, I heard voices coming from the kitchen, causing me to pause. I tipped my head in their direction so that I could hear what they were saying.

"I'm just saying it's a tad strange, my new friend sleeping on your bed," Clementine said. I could hear the accusation in her voice, and it made my entire body prick with embarrassment.

Archer growled. "I told you, I have no idea how she got there. I got home late last night, and when I woke up this morning, I was on the couch and she was in my bed." Archer sounded irritated but also relaxed. Like he was enjoying that this was a mystery that Clementine couldn't solve.

Or that it was irritating her this much.

Not wanting to stand in the shadows and secretly listen to this sibling squabble, I shut his door—loudly— and made my way into the kitchen. Clementine was standing next to the stove with eggs sizzling in the pan.

Archer was standing next to her with a coffee pot in one hand and a mug in the other.

I eyed him for a moment, trying to size him up. Did he remember what he did last night? It was ridiculous, but I was pretty sure the feeling of his arms wrapped around me was burned onto my skin. My ridiculous heart even picked up speed at the thought.

I was having a mental breakdown. I was sure of it.

"Morning," Clementine said with a cheerful tone.

I turned to her and gave her a smile. "Morning." Not sure what I should do—sit down or help—I stood there in the middle of the kitchen.

Thankfully, Clementine seemed to take in my awkwardness and decided to direct me. "Sit," she commanded as she walked over with a spatula in one hand and the hot pan in the other. She bumped me with her hip as she nodded in the direction of the table.

I followed her instructions and settled in at the table. Clementine busied herself with dumping eggs on the plate in front of me as well as the plate next to where I sat. I was about to ask who that was for when the sound of chair legs scraping the floor drew my attention over.

Archer set his mug on the table and plopped down on the chair. "These look great," he said as he began to shovel his food into his mouth.

"Yeah, they look amazing," I said as I tried to ignore the feeling of Archer's elbow as it bumped against mine. I was pretty sure my entire face was bright pink and the last thing I needed was for Clementine to see it and ask me what was wrong.

What I needed to do was finish this breakfast and get out of here as fast as I could. The inn was calling my name, and I was ready to get started fixing it up. Plus, getting away from Archer seemed like a wise idea.

"Wow, you were hungry," Clementine said as she sat down with her own plate and mug of coffee.

I smiled and shrugged. "I guess so."

We all ate in silence for a few moments until Clementine cleared her throat and glanced at Archer and me. "So, starting work on the inn today?" Clementine asked.

I slowed my chewing as I studied her and then responded with a nod.

"Clem," Archer said. His voice was low and threatening.

Clementine pulled an orange out of the bowl in the middle of the table and began to peel it. She shrugged. "What? It's a simple question."

When I peeked over at Archer, he had his eyebrows lowered as he stared at Clementine.

She chuckled. "I've never seen you up this early to start the day. It seems like you're motivated to do something other than hang out on the couch all day." She thrust her thumb in my direction. "Perhaps the thought of a job?"

Archer dropped his fork, and it clattered on his plate. He leaned back and rubbed his hands on his upper thighs. "I apologize for my nosy sister," he said in my direction.

I chuckled. She reminded me so much of Brielle. "It's

okay. I'm used to it." I pushed the last bits of egg around on my plate with my fork. "I'm pretty indecisive most times. I need pushes."

The sound of something crashing to the ground drew our attention. Clementine was the first to react, leaping from her chair and heading in the direction of the sound.

Now alone with Archer, I grabbed a glass of water that Clementine had brought over and downed it. I needed something to do before I decided to open my mouth. With the way my mind was reeling from Archer's proximity, I feared I wouldn't be able to keep myself from speaking.

And bringing up what happened last night.

I was pretty sure that whatever that hug had been wasn't something that sober Archer wanted to talk to me about. It was best to keep my lips sealed. It was never going to happen again anyway.

"So...did you sleep good?" he finally asked just as I began to feel as if the silence was going to slowly suffocate me.

I cleared my throat and nodded. "Yes."

"My bed, it's comfortable, right?"

Heat permeated my cheeks. "Yes," I whispered.

Archer turned to look at me, and for a moment, I felt completely lost in the depths of his brown eyes. He was so close that I was pretty sure I saw gold flecks inside of his irises. I almost leaned forward to get a better look, but then thought better of it.

He drew his eyebrows together, and I could see a question form in his gaze. He wanted to know how I ended up in his room.

Just as I formulated an excuse, my phone chimed. Relief flooded my body as I stood, pushing my chair away from the table, and pulled my phone from my back pocket. "I should get this," I said as I hurried into the living room.

I could feel Archer's gaze on me as I disappeared behind the nearby wall and glanced down at my phone. It was a notification from the delivery people. My mattress was getting dropped off in the next thirty minutes.

Stuffing my phone into my back pocket, I rounded the corner, gathered my dishes together, and set them in the sink. Then I turned and shot Archer an apologetic smile. "I should get going. My bed is being delivered soon."

He was in the midst of chewing as he studied me. Then he stood and brought his dishes over to set them next to mine. "Perfect. I'll give you a ride."

I raised my hand. "No, no. That's okay. Clementine can do it."

He shook his head as he reached past me—brushing his chest against my arm. Flashbacks of the night before raced through my mind. Thankfully, he didn't seem as flustered from my touch as I was from his.

He reappeared with keys in his hand and a determined look in his eye. "It's no problem. Plus, Clem needs to open the store." He threw his keys into the air as he made his way to the front door.

"Come on," he called over his shoulder as he disappeared out onto the landing and headed down the stairs.

I grabbed my purse and bag and then followed after him. There was no backing out of this now. I might as well get into the car with Archer because there should be no reason why it would be awkward. Clementine was my friend, and now Archer was as well.

If I truly believed that the hug last night meant nothing, then being close to Archer—even working with him—shouldn't be a problem.

My head understood this.

My heart?

That was another story.

8

CLEMENTINE

I took it as a good sign when Archer didn't return after he left to drop off Maggie. Hopefully she put him to work, and that effectively got him out of my hair.

Hallelujah.

I still wanted to know how she'd ended up sleeping in his bed, but I figured that would be part of a later conversation. One that could take place out of the view of my brother's dagger-throwing stare.

He wasn't interested in getting to the bottom of it. But I was.

Dad had dropped one of his dresser drawers on the floor, so I spent the morning helping him clean his room back up. He was convinced that the Vietnamese had hid bombs in his room, and he was determined to root them out.

By the time I was able to calm him down and reorganize his room, he was passed out on his bed. After covering him up, I left him to sleep while I hurried downstairs and opened the store.

Even though my morning was exhausting, I still had a spring in my step. Maggie being here certainly shook up my life, but maybe that was what I needed. A change of pace from the monotony that my life had become.

Around noon, the door opened and Shari's familiar voice filled the store. I glanced up from where I was perched on my stool. Shari was a few years older than me, but ever since I dated her brother, Jake, we'd been best friends.

Even after Jake broke my heart when he left to pursue fishing in Alaska—but that wasn't something I allowed myself to think about.

"Shar!" I called out as I jumped from my seat and hurried around the corner.

Shari's hair was windblown and her cheeks pink as she ushered Tag and Bella over to me. They were both whining about being in the "boring store," and Shari was trying to shush them.

I dropped down so I was eye level with them. "Boring?" I asked as I reached out to poke their sides.

They both erupted into a fit of giggles as they twisted and turned in an attempt to get away from me.

"Did I just hear you call Auntie Clem's store *boring*?"

Bella settled first and looked at me with her big blue eyes. Ones that matched her mom's—and, when I allowed myself to think of him, Jake's. She furrowed her brow.

"You have no toys," she said as she folded her arms across her chest.

I reached out and hoisted her onto my hip. "No toys?" I asked as I walked over to the counter and fished out one of the caramels that I'd confiscated from Archer's reach.

She squealed and eagerly unwrapped it. She shoved it into her mouth and then fished one out for Tag. They looked happy as they stood there, slurping and chomping on their candy.

Now that they were distracted, I turned my attention over to Shari, who looked tired. She was not only the vice principal at the school, but I was pretty sure that she was going through a rough time with Craig, her husband and the sheriff of Magnolia.

"How are things?" I asked as I leaned against the counter and gave her a soft smile.

She sighed and blew out her breath. A strand of her dark hair flew up and then landed back on her face. "Craig's working again. So I'm on kid duty."

I reached into the container and fished out a caramel. I handed it over to her. "You look like you need this," I said with a smile.

She took the candy and shot me a thankful expression. She looked thoughtful as she chewed on it. "Did you hear that someone moved into Magnolia Inn?"

I nodded. Tag and Bella had finished their candy and were revving up to start complaining again. I grabbed both of their hands and led them over to Spencer's corner of the store. He was big and gruff, but he adored kids—especially these two.

They would follow him around his work area, asking him questions and giggling as he allowed them to use the drill. After I dropped them off, I waved Shari over to the register, and we sat down on the stools behind it. I could see Shari's shoulders drop as her body relaxed into the seat.

"I can take the kids; you know this," I said.

Shari glanced over and offered me a weak smile. "I know. I just feel bad. You have Archer. Your dad." She raised her eyebrows.

I waved away her reaction. I wasn't interested in starting that up again. Shari wasn't shy about her desire for me to put Dad in a home. She said he would be safer and I would be happier. But I couldn't see that. How was deserting my dad going to make me happy?

Every time I thought about it, a rock settled in my stomach, and I wanted to vomit. I took that as a bad sign and wrote off all the doctors and friends who said otherwise.

"I can handle it," I scoffed as I reached out to mindlessly shuffle some paper around.

Shari made a sound that resembled *mm-hmm*, but when I turned around to protest, her lips were pinched shut and she had an innocent look on her face. I shot her a glare.

"Maggie's nice. You should come to the inn with me to meet her," I said.

Shari's expression fell again as her gaze shifted to the large windows in the front of the store. I could see her pain. It was written across her face. I wished she'd open up to me about Craig, but she was pretty tight-lipped about their relationship. She was determined to face whatever she was going through alone, and it killed me that she felt like that.

"We'll see." She glanced back over at me. "What time are you heading over there?"

"Probably after I get off of work. I feel bad, but I kind of pushed her to hire Archer." I raised my eyebrows. "I was worried that our couch would fuse to his butt with how much he sat on that thing. Plus, he needs to start creating a life for himself."

"So you pushed your brother off on the newcomer?" Shari tsked as she shook her head.

I winced, realizing that it probably hadn't been the smartest thing, but what else could I do? Maggie needed the help, and my brother needed something in his life other than me.

Pushing away the guilt that had risen up inside of me, I shrugged. "She'll be fine. He'll be fine." My voice trailed off as I muttered, "I'll be fine."

"Well, be prepared for her to kick him out," Shari said as she slipped off the chair and called for Tag and Bella, who let out a collective groan. "I came in for lightbulbs, and you distracted me," she said as she waggled her finger in my direction.

I pointed toward the back. "Second aisle on your right."

She nodded. "I know." Then she disappeared. Tag and Bella came over, and I entertained them until Shari got back and purchased her items. I walked them to the front door and waved through the window as they disappeared around the building.

I sighed as I allowed my gaze to soften and my mind to clear. Then, for some reason, my mind drifted to Jake and my entire body began to ache.

We'd dated all of high school and were planning on heading to New York for college. But then Dad got sick and Jake got a job on a lobster boat, and suddenly, the plans we'd made for ourselves were no longer feasible. I wasn't going to move to Alaska, and he wasn't going to stay here.

I wanted to say that our breakup was amicable, but it didn't feel that way. Not when my heart still hurt when I thought about him—when I allowed myself to feel the emotions that I'd buried so long ago.

When I allowed those, I knew I wasn't okay. I was always going to miss him. No matter what.

I pushed off the window and wandered over to the register. Thankfully, business picked up, and I didn't have a moment to disappear into the past again.

By seven, the store was cleared out. I walked over to the front door and locked it, flipping the sign to closed. I hurried to cash out the machine and dump that day's receipts onto my desk in the back office. Once I flipped off the lights, I hurried upstairs to find Dad sitting in front of the TV with the volume a few clicks too loud.

I grabbed the remote and adjusted the volume. I was going to feed him and get him into bed. Then I was going to head over to Maggie's.

From the lack of my brother cemented to the couch, I realized that he hadn't come back yet. Either Maggie had him working, or he had disappeared to the pub again. Which I wouldn't put past my brother.

After heating Dad's dinner in the microwave, I set it in front of him on a TV tray and hurried into my room to change. I threw on a t-shirt and shorts and pulled my hair up into a ponytail.

When I got back, Dad had finished off his food, and I was able to convince him to retire to his room with little to no objection.

Win.

After I helped him change into his pajamas, I tucked him into bed with the remote next to him. The news was on, but he was barely watching. As soon as his head hit the pillow, his eyes drifted closed.

I kissed him on the forehead, told him I'd be back, and left.

Thankfully, I'd installed cameras in his room, so I could keep tabs on him while I was out. He wasn't much of a mover though, and once he was in his bed, he was out for the night.

Which was good. I was ready to head over to Maggie's for a break.

I texted Archer as I made my way toward my car. I told him I'd be over there in fifteen. He didn't respond, but I didn't think too much of it. After all, he was working, which was a good sign. He needed to feel useful again.

Or he was flat-out drunk at the pub. Either way, I was going to find out in about ten minutes.

I grabbed a pizza from the diner on my way over. I hadn't eaten all day, and I was starving. I figured I'd share or eat it all myself.

I pulled into Magnolia Inn's parking lot, killed the engine, and opened the door. I shoved my purse strap onto my shoulder, gripped the pizza box in my hand, and made my way across the lot and up the stairs.

The house seemed quiet. The sun had set, and the moon was shining above, reflecting off the ocean and the evening waves. I took in a deep breath of the salty air and knocked.

A few seconds later, the door opened, and Maggie's confused expression filled the opening. I held up the pizza box, and a smile spread across her face. "You're a life-saver," she said as she pushed the door open and let me in.

There were no lights on. Instead, I could see the flicker of candles from the kitchen. I made my way into the room and set the pizza down on the counter.

"How did today go?" I asked as I began checking the cupboards for plates. When I kept coming up empty-handed, Maggie produced some paper ones. After I dished up the pizza, we settled down on the floor of the dining room and began to eat.

"It was good. We got some work done. Archer spent most of his time over the bridge getting supplies."

I pulled the pizza from my lips, cheese stretching out as I did. Finally, I had to break the string with my finger and then set the slice down as I chewed thoughtfully. "So he stayed, huh?"

Maggie sighed, and nodded as she stretched out on the floor with her hands behind her and her legs extended in front. "Yep. I figured if he's willing to work, I'll take his help. He even started a list of guys on the island that can help out." She glanced around. "I'm good at the decorations, not so good at knowing what's a solid foundation or not."

I nodded as I took another bite. "Archer's good for that. He's smarter than he lets on. He went to Yale back when he and Collette were still together." I chewed as I glanced around.

When Maggie didn't respond, I glanced over to see her studying me. "Collette?" she asked.

I nodded and then winced. Archer was not going to be happy that I was discussing his past with Maggie. He didn't like talking to me about it, much less strangers. "But don't tell him I said something. He'd kill me."

Maggie held up her hands. "I won't." Then she drew up her legs, wrapping her arms around them, and rested her chin on her knees. "He's not much of a talker, is he?" she asked.

I snorted as I grabbed another piece of pizza. "Archer? No. Never has been. And since the accident—" I bit my tongue before more Archer information spilled from my lips. It was one thing to talk about my issues—which there were a few—but it was a whole other thing to talk about Archer's. He was private and would not like it if I spilled his problems to just anyone.

"Does it have to do with Elise?" Maggie asked, her voice quiet as if she wasn't sure if she should ask.

Taken aback, I stared at her. "Archer told you about her?"

Maggie reached out and drew circles on the floor with her finger. "Not so much told. More like mumbled to me last night."

I set my pizza down. "Does this have to do with you moving from the couch to his bed?"

She nodded. "We didn't do anything, I swear. He just came home in the middle of the night and sat on me. When I finally got him off, he was mumbling about being forgiven and Elise." She rubbed her arm with her hand.

I sighed as I extended an arm behind me and put my body weight on it. I tipped my face toward the ceiling. To say that I missed my niece was an understatement. What happened to her was tragic. But it had been an accident—even if Archer wanted to blame himself for it.

"Elise was his daughter. She passed away," I said softly as I closed my eyes. Her death five years ago had been hell. I'd never seen my big, strong older brother brought to his knees before. Elise had gone missing, and by the time they found her, she'd crawled into the neighbor's hot tub and drowned.

My entire body went cold as I leaned forward and wrapped my arms around my chest. I hated thinking or talking about it. I was good at pushing those feelings way down where they couldn't resurface.

Where they couldn't hurt me again.

"I'm so sorry," Maggie whispered. When I glanced over at her, I saw her sympathetic gaze as she offered me a small smile. "That had to be hard."

I cleared my throat, hoping to dislodge the emotions that had set up camp there, and nodded. "No one took it as hard as Archer did. He's been a mess ever since."

Maggie nodded. "I bet."

I forced my happiness to the surface. That's where I liked to live. With Dad's disease and Elise's death, too many horrible things had happened to me. I was drowning, and the only way I could get up every morning was by telling myself that I was happy.

Even if I was pretty sure I couldn't remember what happiness felt like.

Maggie collected our plates and stood. "Well, I'm happy that Archer wants to help me. With his assistance, this project will get done a lot faster."

I nodded as I stood and followed her. "I can help, too," I offered.

Maggie smiled. "That would be amazing."

"And if you don't mind two wild kids running around, Shari would help as well."

Maggie furrowed her brow. "Shari?"

I nodded. "She's like my older sister of sorts. She's got

kids and a husband but is always looking for stuff to do." I rested my forearms on the counter in front of me and leaned my weight on them. "Her husband is the sheriff here."

Maggie threw away the plates and then turned. "That would be awesome. The more hands the better."

I drummed on the countertop and nodded. "Everyone's excited to see this place restored to its former glory. And having someone new move in is nice too."

Maggie sighed as she glanced out the window. "You know, I didn't think I needed it, but the change in scenery seems to be just what I needed too."

I laughed. "Better than New York?"

She grinned back at me. "Way better."

We spent the next hour talking until I couldn't keep exhaustion at bay anymore. I said goodbye to Maggie and headed back home, where I checked on Dad and fell asleep—fully clothed—on my bed.

9

MAGGIE

I woke up the next morning refreshed and ready to tackle the day. If I were honest with myself, I was ready to see Archer again.

Even though yesterday he'd spent most of his time here either outside, surveying the work that needed to be done, or across the bridge getting supplies, I enjoyed the fact that he was here and I wasn't alone.

We'd kept our conversation pretty light, but there was one point where I made a joke and he smiled. It felt juvenile, but it actually made me giddy.

After my conversation with Clementine, I was beginning to understand more about why he was reserved. Why he'd drunkenly hugged me in the living room. Despite Clementine's willingness to be open with me, I still had so many questions.

I wanted to know more about him.

I hurried to get dressed in a white t-shirt and jean

shorts. I pulled my hair up into a bun on top of my head and slipped my tennis shoes on. We were going to tackle cleaning the siding so we could find the damaged parts, and then Archer was going to replace them.

Once I was ready, I wandered into the kitchen to make a pot of coffee and a quick breakfast. I grabbed the pot and moved to the sink, turning on the faucet. Nothing came out for a moment, and then, in the blink of an eye, water began to spray everywhere.

I yelped as my entire front was soaked. I blinked as I tried to push the water from my eyes. Thankfully, I'd managed to hold onto the coffee pot. If I'd dropped it, it would have most definitely shattered. The last thing I needed was to be blindly walking around shards of glass.

I leaned forward and moved to flip the water off when the flow sputtered and died to nothing.

Sighing, I turned the handle tightly to off and then felt around for a towel.

"That was...entertaining," Archer's deep voice said from behind me.

I yelped and turned. My focus came back, and I could see him standing in the middle of the kitchen with an amused expression. I finally found the towel hanging from the oven door and dabbed my face. Thankfully, the water had been cold, which was helping to cool my skin that had heated from embarrassment.

Once I'd dried most of my skin, I lowered my hands to study him. "So you just watched me get pelted by water?" I asked as I glared at him.

He laughed. "I was on my way to tell you that George is here to look at the plumbing, but you must have not heard me. Once you turned the water on, it was game over."

I wiped my neck as I studied him. "George?"

Archer folded his arms and leaned against the counter. "Yeah. He's a friend from over the bridge. He had a few hours and knows old houses. He offered to come take a look."

"Ah," I said as I moved to wipe my arms.

Archer was studying me when an awkward expression passed over his face. He cleared his throat and straightened. "Um, you…" He nodded toward me.

I studied him. What was he trying to say? "I what?" I asked as I began to feel my face. Did I have something there? I was pretty sure water went up my nose, and the last thing I needed was to have snot all over my face.

Archer's cheeks flushed as he waved to my chest. "You got wet and…I can see…" Each word came out achingly slow, and it wasn't until I glanced down and saw my very black bra showing through my soaked shirt that I understood what he was trying to say.

I yelped and wrapped my arms around my chest. "Oh my gosh," I whispered as I turned and fled to my room. Once I got there, I made my way into the bathroom to inspect the damage.

I'd been right. Everything was showing. My bra. My belly. The top of my pants. The shirt had literally turned see-through from the water.

I shook my head as I pulled it off and changed into a black shirt. With the embarrassment that was coursing through me, I would have pulled out a nun's outfit if I had it. Why I ever thought wearing a white shirt when we were going to work on the siding was a good idea baffled my mind.

Once I was changed, I fixed my hair and my makeup and finally went back out to the kitchen. The smell of breakfast filled the air. I rounded the corner to find Archer standing in front of the stove, stirring eggs in a pan.

"You didn't have to," I said just as the coffee machine dinged.

Archer shrugged as he grabbed my one mug and filled it. "I was here. Figured I'd help you out." He glanced over at me, and his half smile caused my heart rate to pick up.

I blinked a few times and then turned and focused on grabbing a plate for the eggs. With one in hand, I turned to find him standing behind me with the pan and spatula. He didn't speak as he dumped the eggs onto my plate and then handed me a fork.

"Thanks," I said softly as I moved over to the nearby counter, set the plate down, and began to eat. It was so strange, being in this small town. Everyone seemed to help everyone else.

I was not used to this. I'd lived in New York for a long time before I even met Brielle. I'd been alone with Sean. I hadn't even been here a week, and I already knew more people than I had living in a big city.

"Does it not taste okay?" Archer asked me as he bent down and caught my gaze.

I was chewing and hadn't noticed him studying me. "I'm sorry?" I asked as I quickly swallowed.

"The eggs. Do they not taste good?" he asked again.

I glanced down at the plate and then back up to him. "They taste great. Why would you think they don't?"

He chuckled as he folded his arms and leaned against the counter again. "You have a strange look on your face. I was worried I messed them up."

I shoveled another forkful of eggs into my mouth just to prove what I'd said. "They're great," I said after swallowing them. I set my fork down. "I was just thinking about how different a small town is compared to a city."

Archer ran his hands through his hair. "Yeah, it is. And since Magnolia is an island, it's even smaller." He blew out his breath. "Which can be a good thing or a bad thing."

My thoughts turned to Elise, and I wondered if he was referring to that or something else. Did Elise die here? Had he lived off the island?

"You have experience?" I asked as I picked up my fork and continued eating.

Archer nodded. "I lived in New Haven for four years while I got my degree at Yale and then spent another three years at law school. I didn't come back to Magnolia until..." A sorrowful expression passed over his face as his voice drifted off. He straightened and clenched his fists as he peered out the window.

I could see the pain of his past. It was etched into his

features and body language. He was hurting, and hurting was something I understood. I may have never lost a child, but I was divorced. I knew the pain of loss.

"Well, I'm sure Clementine's happy you are back," I offered as I finished off the eggs and dumped the paper plate into the garbage. "It seems like she wants what's best for you."

Archer nodded. "She's always taking care of people. Did you know she had a full-ride to Juilliard for dance?" He peered over his shoulder at me.

"Really?"

Archer sighed. "But Dad got sick, and she stayed. Didn't want me to give up on my dream, so she took on the burden of taking care of our dad." He dropped his gaze to his hands and stood there in silence.

Not sure if I should speak or not, I decided to wait until he continued.

"She's like that though. Pushy, yes, but she has a good heart. She wants what's best for people."

The affection in his voice caused goosebumps to erupt all over my body. It showed a softer side of Archer that I was beginning to realize hid underneath his prickly top layer.

"I get that," I said with a smile as I stepped up to stand next to him. "She seems like a caretaker." She'd definitely taken it upon herself to take care of me since the moment I set foot on this island. And with my history of bad choices, I was more than willing to let someone else take control for a while.

"Yeah." He released that word slowly, as if it held a lot of meaning, before he turned to me and met my gaze. "She's been taking care of me since I can remember. Which is sad, seeing how I'm the oldest." His voice trailed off as he held my gaze for a moment before he nodded. "I'm going to go check on George. If he's got your plumbing figured out, we can get started."

I nodded, but Archer didn't wait for my response. Instead, he took a few long steps to the back door, pulled it open, and disappeared outside.

Once he was gone, I blew out my breath as I folded my arms and leaned against the nearby counter. I allowed my gaze to soften as my thoughts returned to Archer and our conversation.

It was strange how connected I felt to someone I'd just met. When he talked, he sounded and looked just as lost as I felt. When his gaze met mine, I could see his pain and heartache. It was similar to the ache inside of myself.

Was it possible that we could both be so lost? Like two ships in the darkness, both searching for that beam of light to guide us. I knew it sounded corny and ridiculous, but coming to Magnolia didn't feel like a happenstance anymore. It was almost like I was meant to be here.

Was it my grandmother calling me here? Did I really believe in fate like that?

Because right now, Magnolia seemed pretty perfect.

Feeling like an idiot, I pushed off the counter and headed out the door after Archer. As soon as I stepped out into the sunlight, I raised my hand over my eyes and glanced around.

The ocean was glistening in the warm sun. A soft breeze picked up and surrounded me. I made my way off the porch and glanced up at the house. What had seemed so hopeless just a few days ago was suddenly beautiful. I couldn't wait to get my hands on the siding and spruce it up.

This inn felt like a representation of myself, and I was determined to find its beauty no matter what.

I started walking toward Archer and George. They shook hands, and George turned to walk toward the front. I followed him with my gaze as I furrowed my brow. Once he was gone, I turned my attention to Archer.

"What did he say?" I asked.

Archer's face was stoic for a moment before he clapped his hands together and his frown morphed into a smile. "He said he fixed the issue. The pipes were good, just needed to be flushed. We should be up and running."

I couldn't help the cheer that erupted. Not only did it mean we could get started, but it also meant I could actually shower here. I raised my hand for a high five, and Archer stared at it.

Feeling like a dork, I shrugged, but as I started to lower my hand, Archer slapped it. It was awkward, but I was always awkward, so what was new? He chuckled as he nodded toward the hose he'd left on the lawn. "I'll get this hooked up, and we can get started."

I whooped and clapped my hands. Heat permeated my

body when I realized how dorky I looked. Archer didn't seem to mind as he walked over to the hose, began to unwind it, and pulled it over to the spigot on the side of the house.

Get a grip, Maggie, I scolded myself.

If I was going to survive this remodel, I needed to stop making a fool of myself.

Thankfully, once the water started flowing and the soap was out, Archer and I didn't have time to talk, which meant I didn't have time to embarrass myself. Except for that moment when I slipped on the mud and *almost* crashed to the ground only to save myself at the last moment, I was accident-free.

Archer had picked up these car washing brushes when he went across the bridge, and they worked wonders as I scrubbed the areas I could reach. Thankfully, the inn had wraparound decks on each level, which meant I didn't have to climb a ladder to get to the top.

I was completely soaked when I turned the hose off and declared that it was lunch time. Archer was working on a different side and must have not heard me, because a moment later, he rounded the house...shirtless.

I was so caught off guard that all I could do was stand there and stare. It was the morning in his room all over again. His hair was damp and had begun to curl at the ends. His skin glistened in the sun.

He met my gaze and furrowed his brow as if asking me what I was staring at. Embarrassment flushed my skin as I dropped my gaze and cleared my throat. "I figured we should break for lunch?" I said. My brain was really short-circuiting right now.

From the corner of my eye, I saw Archer nod.

"I'm on board. I'm gonna grab some dry clothes from my truck. Meet out front in ten?"

I nodded, and he turned to head around the inn. Realizing that I had very little food, I called out, "Lunch in town?"

He paused and glanced over his shoulder. "Sounds good."

When he left, I exhaled and tipped my face toward the sky. There was something seriously wrong with me. How could I lose all control of my mind and my body when I saw Archer sans shirt?

I was a grown woman. I had self-control. I'd just misplaced it.

I grumbled to myself all the way into the house and into my room. I changed into a flowy summer dress and fixed my hair. By the time I felt somewhat presentable, I realized that I was four minutes late. I grabbed my purse and hurried through the inn and out the front door.

Archer was leaning on the deck railing with his hands in his front pockets, staring out at the ocean. His hair had mostly dried and was shifting in the breeze. He looked so calm it was almost picturesque.

Feeling as if I were intruding, I stood still and dropped my gaze. It only took a few seconds for me to realize it was creepier for me to quietly stand here than it would be for me to just speak. By the time I figured that out, though, Archer's footsteps drew my attention upward.

Thankfully, he didn't look creeped out. He had on this sexy half smile that sent my pulse racing again.

"Ready?" he asked.

Deciding that talking was probably the stupidest thing I could do right then, I nodded and followed after him. Just as I began rifling around in my purse for my keys, Archer shook his head and threw his own up in the air.

"I'll drive," he said.

Not wanting to argue, I nodded and offered him a soft smile. He opened his door, and I did the same. Once we were settled, Archer started the engine and pulled out of the parking lot.

We rode in silence all the way to the diner. It was nice just sitting there, not feeling the need to speak. With Sean, silence meant he was mad at me. I always felt like I needed to speak to keep him entertained.

Not Archer. He seemed completely content with the quiet. His wrist was resting on the steering wheel while his other elbow was out the open window. Johnny Cash's rough voice droned from the speakers and filled the cab.

I found my entire body relaxing as I turned my gaze outward. It had been a long time since I'd felt so at peace.

Magnolia was rapidly becoming my home.

For the first time, I felt like I belonged.

The fact that Penny had every intention of selling the inn was becoming a distant memory. Besides, if she saw this place—saw how happy I was here—she'd keep it.

At least, that was my hope.

10

CLEMENTINE

I t was dark when Archer, looking exhausted, finally rolled into the house. His skin was pink, and his gaze was tired as he nodded at me and then headed straight for the bathroom. Not wanting him to escape until he gave me an update on the inn and Maggie, I scrambled up from the puzzle I was half-heartedly working on at the table and headed over to him.

"How did it go?" I asked as I fell into step with him.

Archer cast me a sidelong glance as he groaned. "I stink and I'm tired. Can we play twenty questions later?" He was in the bathroom now, pulling his shirt off while trying to shut the door.

I stuck my hand out. He wasn't going to get out of speaking to me. "Archer, details."

To be honest, I was worried I'd been too pushy with Maggie ever since she got here. I spent all day in the store worrying that I'd overstepped. I had a habit of running new friends off faster than a rabbit being chased by a fox.

He grumbled again but sighed as he glanced down at me. "What do you want to know?"

I chewed my bottom lip as I collapsed against the bathroom door. "Did you talk about me? Is Maggie annoyed with me? Did you exhaust her? How much work did you get done?"

Archer scoffed as he tipped his head to the side. "Do you actually want me to answer any of these? The twenty questions comment was a joke."

I pinched my lips together and nodded. "Sorry," I whispered.

He chuckled as he reached out and patted my shoulder. "Maggie is nice, and she likes you. I think you'd make a great couple. Write her a note, and I'll pass it to her during P.E. Now, can I please shower?"

I shot him an annoyed look. Of course he was going to mock me. It was Archer's specialty. But then, realization dawned on me. It had been a while since I'd seen Archer this happy. Or heard that familiar teasing tone to his voice.

My eyes filled with tears, and I felt like an idiot standing there, on the brink of a sobbing fest, while my brother looked at me with desperation because he wanted some privacy.

But the hope that my brother was back overwhelmed me so much that I pulled him into a bear hug.

"Clem—" he stammered.

I kept my arms tightly wrapped around him. "I've missed you."

I could hear Archer's laugh as it rumbled in his chest. His arms felt familiar as they wrapped around me, and he gave me his signature squeeze complete with a quick lift off the ground.

"I've only been gone since this morning," he said as he stepped back and held me at arm's length, as if he was worried I'd hug him again.

I nodded and smiled at him. I'd let him think that was what I meant. He'd been so distant for so long that I'd doubted I was ever going to be able to get him back. Seeing him now was like seeing the sun peeking through the clouds after a long summer rain.

It was refreshing and hopeful.

Realizing that I was just standing there with what I could only assume was a goofy look on my face, I pinched my nose, hoping to break the tension. "Ew, yeah, you should shower."

"Har, har," Archer said as he rested his hands on my shoulder and pushed me out of the bathroom. "Maggie really does like you. I think you've found a lifelong friend," he said before he shut the door.

I paused as I let his words sink in. Then I pumped my fist into the air as I walked through the hallway to Dad's room. After checking on him to make sure he was asleep, I collapsed onto the couch, picked up the remote, and selected the Korean drama I'd been watching earlier.

The fact that my neurotic self hadn't scared her off meant Archer was right. I'd found a friend.

————

The next morning, I dressed and packed a picnic for that evening. It was my day off—Michelle, my part time helper, was working—which meant that I was going to go with Archer to the inn and spend time helping Maggie. I was excited to get out of the house, feel the salty wind on my face, and get my body moving.

Dad and I were sitting at the table as I anxiously waited for Archer to emerge from his bedroom. Dad had already eaten breakfast, and I'd called Mrs. Swanson, an old friend of my parents, to see if she could come spend some time with Dad.

She agreed, stating that she would "bring her knitting and entertain Dirk." It took a while to get her to stop talking long enough for me to thank her and hang up. With Dad taken care of, I was ready for a day that didn't include nuts and bolts or watching Dad snore in his chair.

I was ready to have a day just for myself.

As soon as Archer's door opened, I popped up from my seat with a wide smile. "Ready?" I exclaimed as I rushed over and grabbed his arm and pulled him toward the door.

Archer stumbled as he attempted to follow after me. "What's with you?" he asked as he put his whole weight into pulling back, which stopped me dead in the middle of the kitchen. "I need to eat breakfast," he said as he tried to pivot to the sink.

"I made you a breakfast burrito. Dad was up early today, so I got a lot done."

Archer stared down at me. "And drank all the coffee in the house?" he asked as he reached down and peeled my hands off his arm. He took a few steps over to the sink, where he filled a glass with water.

"I'm just excited," I said. If I were honest with him, yes, I'd already had five cups of coffee this morning. But when you get up at four, what other choice do you have?

Archer said good morning to Dad as he sat down, and they talked for a few minutes. I could tell Dad was tired, so I walked over and knelt down next to him. "Want me to take you to the living room?" I asked.

Dad nodded as he reached out and grabbed my hand. Then he patted it a few times. I helped him stand, and he shuffled over to his chair with my hand still wrapped in his. He sat, and I grabbed a nearby blanket and draped it over him. Just as I turned on the news, a knock sounded on the door.

"Mrs. Swanson," I called to Archer, who was putting his glass in the dishwasher. He waved at me as I pulled open the door to the sunshine smile and wrinkled face of Mrs. Swanson. Her white hair was pulled up into a bun at the top of her head, and her readers were perched on the tip of her nose.

"Hello, Clementine," she said as I stepped to the side and allowed her in. Once she was inside, she paused and ran her gaze over me. "You look more and more like Janet every day."

I gave her a hug. "Thanks." Even though I was adopted, I reveled in those kinds of compliments. It gave me a sense of belonging.

"Now, where is Dirk?" she asked.

I motioned toward the living room, and Mrs. Swanson nodded as she made her way to the couch and sat. She began talking to Dad as if he were listening, but his eyes kept drifting closed. Soon, they were shut completely, but Mrs. Swanson didn't notice. Instead, she was going on and on about her boys and what they were up to.

Now that everything was situated, I turned my attention to Archer. He was sitting on a chair, tying his shoes at what felt like a turtle's pace. I hurried over to him. "Ready?" I asked.

He harrumphed and stood, glaring playfully down at me. "Can we take your enthusiasm down a notch?" he asked.

I shook my head as I grabbed the strap of the cooler and pulled my hair out of the way as I shouldered it. "Nah. I'm just excited to get out of the store for once."

Archer snorted as he called a goodbye to Mrs. Swanson and Dad. Mrs. Swanson replied with a quick wave thrown our direction. I hurried after Archer, shutting the door behind me.

I climbed into the passenger seat of Archer's truck at the same time Archer climbed into the driver's seat. Soon, we were on the road heading toward the inn. I couldn't help but talk, and Archer just listened. There were a few times I caught him smiling. Which was strange. I hadn't seen my brother smile in so long, I'd convinced myself that his face was no longer capable of making that expression.

When we pulled into the inn's parking lot, I unbuckled and jumped down to the ground. After grabbing the cooler, I fell into step with Archer as we made our way up the stairs and across the porch. We stopped at the front door, and Archer knocked.

A few seconds later, Maggie appeared. Her eyes were wide and sparkling as she pulled the door all the way open and waved us in. "Good morning," she said in a breathy voice as if she'd run to get the door.

I smiled at her as I held up the cooler. "Fridge. I brought food so we can have a picnic on the beach."

She nodded and led me into the kitchen, where she opened the fridge door. I took note of her seriously lacking food situation as I shoved the cooler onto one of the wire shelves inside.

"We need to get you some groceries," I declared as I turned around and studied her.

She gave me a sheepish look. "Sorry. Haven't had the time. We've been so busy." She peeked over at Archer, who had followed us into the kitchen and was leaning against the counter.

He had this goofy look on his face that confused me. But he'd been doing a lot of things that confused me lately, why was this look any different?

I shut the fridge door and brushed my hands against each other. "All right, I'm here to work," I said as I rolled my shoulders. "What's the plan for today?"

Maggie smiled. "Well, I was going to start cleaning out the attic. I found some amazing pieces of furniture in there that I think we could clean up and put in the rooms." She eyed me. "Think you could help me with that?"

I stood at attention and saluted her. "Yes ma'am."

Maggie shook her head as she peeked over at Archer. "Are you going to work on the siding?"

Archer nodded. "Yeah. I should be able to finish up today."

"Great. We have jobs. Let's get 'em done."

I clapped my hands and shouted, "Break!" Archer threw me an annoyed look, and Maggie just smiled. I followed after her as she led me up to the third floor. When we got there, the attic door was already open, and a ladder dropped down into the middle of the hallway.

Maggie climbed up, and so did I.

It was dusty in the attic. It made me wonder how long it had been since someone had been up here. The Magnolia Inn had been vacant for as long as I could remember. My mother had been friends with Dorthy and had talked about her occasionally. When Dorthy divorced, she moved from the inn to California, where she lived the rest of her life.

It made the residents of Magnolia sad to see the once iconic inn deteriorate, but Dorthy refused to sell. So it sat, becoming a shadow of what it used to be.

"Aren't these beautiful?" Maggie asked as she ran her hand along a rolltop desk in the corner. There was a small window in the attic through which the sun was pouring through, lighting the space.

The desk she was standing by was a dark oak. I could see the details in the carvings on the drawers and edges. Even through the dust, I could tell it was a beautiful piece.

"Yeah, that's a keeper," I said as I walked over to the desk and fiddled with the brass knobs. I opened the top drawer and peeked inside. Some old papers were still inside.

Curiosity won out, and I wrapped my fingers around them and pulled them out. The paper had yellowed, and they smelled musty. Maggie moved to peek over my shoulder.

"It looks like some old receipts and stuff," I said as I laid the papers out so she could see.

She nodded as she took the top one and studied it. "Do you think this is my grandmother's writing?" she asked as she ran her fingertips across the elegant cursive.

"Probably," I said. Then a name caught my eye. Dorthy Addington's signature marked the bottom of the invoice she was looking at. "At least, that is," I said pointing to the signature.

"Wow," she breathed.

"Did you not know her?"

Maggie snorted. "I barely know my own mother," she said as she picked up another piece of paper.

I pulled open another drawer and removed its

contents. Just as I moved to close the drawer, something caught my eye. I reached toward the back and pulled out what looked like a photo.

"Look at this," I said as I tipped it toward her. The picture had faded, and it definitely looked dated, but I recognized a few things in the photo. A group of women were sitting on the front steps of the inn. I could pick out my mother in the midst of the women there. She looked younger. Her hair was dark, and she had on a flowy dress.

Her arm was wrapped around another woman's shoulders, and they were all holding a book in their arms.

"Who are these women?" Maggie asked as she gently took the photo from me.

"Well, that's my mom," I said as I reached over and pointed.

Maggie nodded, and a few seconds later, she turned the photo over. "Me and the girls. First meeting of The Red Stiletto Book Club," she read.

The cursive looked the same as on the paperwork we'd been inspecting.

"Me and the girls? Do you think that's your grandmother?" I asked.

Maggie shrugged. "I don't know. I've never seen a photo of her."

I tapped my chin, wondering who in this town would know. My thoughts turned to Dad, but most times, he thought I was Mom. And then I realized that Mrs. Swanson would know. She'd grown up in this town, and there wasn't a person she didn't remember, even if they only lived here during tourist season.

"Come on, I think I know who could tell us," I said as I grabbed her hand and pulled her toward the opening of the attic.

Once we got outside, we found Archer standing next to a table saw. He had his baseball cap on backwards and was in the midst of lining up a board. He must have heard our footsteps on the gravel because he glanced over at us with his brow furrowed.

"Where are you two going?" he asked.

I waved away his question. "We're on a mission," I said without stopping.

Maggie didn't seem as determined as I did. Instead, she shrugged and said, "We're going to find out who's in this photo," she said as she held up our discovery.

Archer looked confused but just nodded and returned to what he was doing.

The ride home felt as if it was going to take forever. I drummed my fingers on the steering wheel as I drove. Maggie was chatting about her excitement, and I couldn't help but feel the same way.

And the idea that her mom and my grandma might have been friends? Even better.

I pulled into the back parking lot of the hardware store and pulled my key from the ignition. Maggie followed after me as I led her up the back stairs and into the apartment.

Mrs. Swanson was right where I left her, with Dad

snoring in his chair. She must not have heard me come in because she startled when I approached.

She clutched her chest as she let out her breath. "Oh my stars," she said. "You scared me."

I held up my hands. "I'm sorry," I said as I sat down on the couch.

Mrs. Swanson patted my hands. "It's all right, dear. I have a pacemaker for a reason."

Maggie sat down on the coffee table in front of us and gave Mrs. Swanson a soft smile. "Hi," she said.

Mrs. Swanson moved her gaze to studied her, and a moment later, she gasped. "Well, you look like the spitting image of an old friend," she said as she focused back on her knitting.

"I do?" Maggie asked.

Mrs. Swanson nodded. "Yes. She used to own the inn years ago. She upped and moved to California never to be seen again." She sighed as she tipped her face upward, and a soft expression spread across her face. "I do miss Dorthy."

I glanced over at Maggie, whose eyebrows were raised. Our gazes met, and she mouthed, "Oh my gosh!" I laughed. I was used to being mistaken for my mom. From the look on Maggie's face, she was not.

"Mrs. Swanson, could you tell us who's in this photo?" I asked as I nodded at Maggie to hand it over.

Mrs. Swanson adjusted her glasses as she took the photo from Maggie and studied it. "Well, I haven't seen this photo in so long," she said as she brushed her fingers against the people in the picture.

"You've seen this picture before?" I asked as I leaned in.

Mrs. Swanson glanced over at me. "Seen it? I'm in it." She pointed to a short, stocky woman in the back. Her hair was cut into a bob with bangs, and she had wide-rimmed glasses resting on her nose. "That's me," she said.

Then she slipped her finger over. "That's Janet. Your mother," she said as she moved to pat my knee.

"And this," she said as she pointed to the woman whose arm was around my mother. "Is Dorthy. She created the book club. Even made us wear those ridiculous shoes."

I glanced to their feet to see that they were all wearing red stilettos.

"I had a dickens of a time walking in those," she said as she laughed.

I smiled as I glanced up at Maggie, whose eyes were wide as she studied Mrs. Swanson. It was like she was absorbing her words as quickly as she could.

"We met every month at the inn. We read books, yes, but it was more a time for us to spend together. We ate"— she lowered her voice—"we drank. It was a good time." Glancing up, she studied me and then Maggie. "Where did you find this?"

Maggie cleared her throat as she reverently took the photo back from Mrs. Swanson. "In a rolltop desk in the attic of the inn."

Mrs. Swanson smiled. "You're fixing up the inn?"

I leaned in. "Maggie is Dorthy's granddaughter. She's here to fix it up."

Mrs. Swanson parted her lips as she focused on Maggie. "Oh that's wonderful." She extended out her hand. "Octavia Swanson," she said.

Maggie shook her hand. "Maggie."

Mrs. Swanson smiled. "Once the inn is up and working, will you let me know? I'd love to have my son Bob and and his wife Sylvia come down to stay."

"Of course."

I stood up and waved toward the door. "Well, we should get going. We've got a lot of work to do."

Maggie walked next to me, and just as we moved to shut the door behind us, Mrs. Swanson's voice caused us to stop.

"That inn changes lives, just so you know," she called out.

I glanced over at Maggie, who smiled at me. We thanked Mrs. Swanson and then headed out to my car. Just as I climbed in and buckled my seatbelt, I glanced over to see Maggie hugging the photo tightly to her chest.

I knew of one life that the inn seemed to be changing, and she was sitting next to me.

"Ready?" I asked.

Maggie nodded. "Ready."

11

MAGGIE

Clementine and I spent the rest of the morning clearing out the attic. It was comical to try and lower the furniture through the hole in the ceiling, so we brought down all the little items we could and then went off to find Archer to help us with the rest.

My mind was swirling from our discovery, so I had a hard time concentrating. It didn't help that Archer had decided that shirts were optional and had removed his hours ago. It was hard not to stare as his muscles rippled while we lowered the furniture down to his waiting arms.

I didn't blame him; I was sweating like a stuck pig. I hadn't had the air conditioning checked out, and today the temperatures were nearing ninety inside the inn. I'd opened the windows, but that did very little to cool the air around us.

"Where do you want me to put this?" Archer called up to me.

I moved to the opening of the attic to see him standing there with sweat on his brow. His dark hair was curling around the edges again, and he moved to push it off his forehead. My heart took off racing, and I mentally shushed it. The last thing I needed was Clementine hearing my ridiculous reaction.

Plus, liking Archer went against my goal to never look at another man again. I'd come to Magnolia in such a good headspace, and I didn't want to negate all my positive self-talk by falling for the first guy I met.

Romance and I were just not meant to get along.

"Just put it in one of the empty rooms," I said as I waved down the hallway. "I'm going to clean them up tonight to see what is salvageable and what isn't."

He glanced in the direction I motioned and then back up to me. He gave me a quick nod and then reached down and heaved the dresser up.

Cue heart pounding as I watched him disappear from sight.

"I'm beat," Clementine said as she sat down on the ground and extended her legs out in front of her.

I nodded as I gathered the last few items by the opening so I could hurry and hand them down to Archer. If the house was hot, the attic felt ten times hotter. I was ready to get out of there.

Thankfully, Archer seemed just as motivated to finish that attic as we were, and ten minutes later, I waited as Clementine climbed down the ladder. Once she was solidly on the ground, I started making my way down.

Just as I neared the middle, my foot slipped, and suddenly I was falling toward the ground. I heard Clementine gasp, but it was as if I were frozen. I couldn't move as I mentally braced myself for impact...but it didn't come.

Instead, I felt two strong arms—the very arms I'd been watching all day—wrap around me and pull me to their owner's chest. I let out my breath as I slammed my eyes shut and stood there, wrapped in Archer's arms.

"Are you okay?" he asked. It might have been my imagination—or desire—but I was pretty sure that Archer's voice had lowered since the last time I heard him speak.

Embarrassment coursed through my body as I stood there with my eyes closed. I couldn't believe I had fallen like that. Not only because Archer now knew how much of a klutz I was, but also because he was now privy to how much I weighed. As a woman who hated the scale, that was the last thing I wanted.

"Thanks," I mumbled as I gathered myself together and pushed away from his chest. His fingers lingered on my skin for a moment before I opened my eyes in time to see him step back.

"You could be dehydrated. You should get some water," he said. His voice had turned gruff, and he didn't stick around. Instead, he pushed his hands through his hair as he jogged down the stairs and out of sight.

"Are you okay?" Clementine asked as she appeared in front of me. She raked her gaze over me and then nodded. "You should get some water. You look really flushed."

I nodded, grateful for the heat for the first time that day. No need to alert Clementine to what her brother's presence had done to me. Plus, it was nothing. It wasn't Archer per se. It was just that it had been a long time since a guy touched me. My body wasn't sure how to process it.

After a few glasses of water, I felt better. Archer declared that he was going to go out and finish up the siding, and Clementine and I decided to tackle the bedrooms. I wanted to get the floors cleaned and the walls wiped down so I could assess what repairs were needed.

I wanted to keep the charm of the old wallpaper and floors, but from what I could tell, there had been water damage in half the rooms. I hoped with a good sanding and new stain, the floors could be salvaged. If I needed to strip the walls, I would, but I didn't want to.

Wallpaper was a headache that I didn't want to deal with.

By dinnertime, Clementine and I had finished half the rooms, and I was about ready to drop from exhaustion. I shuffled into the kitchen and collapsed against the counter. Clementine was on the phone with Mrs. Swanson. From what I could gather, Clementine's dad was asleep and Mrs. Swanson was leaving for the day.

After drinking a glass of water, I wrapped my arms around my chest and closed my eyes. I was ready to eat some dinner and relax. Even though I was physically spent, I hadn't felt this good in a long time. I had a purpose. A job. It was amazing.

"Tired?" Archer's voice broke through my reverie, and

I startled to see him standing near me. He reached forward and turned on the faucet as he filled up his glass.

"Yes," I said as I rubbed my temples. "But it's a good exhaustion."

Archer nodded as he tipped the rim of the glass to his lips and took a drink. "I agree."

I could feel his gaze on me. Heat pricked my skin as I attempted to keep my focus on the floor. Trying to interpret what he was thinking—or why he was staring at me like he was—wasn't going to end well. The last thing I needed was to attempt to figure any of this out and, in return, ruin the only two relationships I currently had on this island.

I needed to get my crap together. Now.

"I'm starving," Clementine said as she rounded the corner.

I straightened and turned my focus to her. Archer did the same as he finished off his water and set his glass down on the counter. "Same," he said.

Clementine fished the cooler out of the fridge and slung the strap over her shoulder. "I say we eat this down on the beach."

Needing something to do, I gathered up some paper plates and silverware and nodded. "Sounds amazing," I said. I hadn't been down to the beach yet. I could feel the salty breeze on my skin and hear the crash of the waves, but I still hadn't made a trek down there.

Today felt like a perfect day to try something new.

Clementine talked all the way down to the water.

Archer walked along one side of her, and I walked along the other. We both seemed content to listen to her talk. When I briefly glanced over at him, butterflies erupted in my stomach at his soft smile. His gaze was focused on the ground, and he seemed to be at peace.

From what Clementine had told me and from what I'd personally witnessed, this look seemed like it was a rarity. When I first met Archer, he looked in pain. From the expression of his face to the depth of his gaze, he seemed as if he were battling demons deep inside of himself.

So to see him now, smiling as Clementine went on and on about the gossip in town, caused a calm to settle around us.

We picked a spot on the sand that was far enough away from the water that we wouldn't get wet, yet close enough to feel the mist off the waves. Clementine pulled out containers of food and opened them up. She'd brought homemade sandwiches, fruit, and bags of chips.

After we loaded up our plates, we ate in silence, all of us facing the water with our legs outstretched. The sun began to sink behind the horizon, coloring the sky with bright oranges and purples. I took in a deep breath as I finished off my food and then dusted off my hands.

Clementine and I gathered up the food while Archer went off to find some wood for a bonfire. Once everything was packed up, Clem and I walked over to the car and put the cooler inside. Clementine disappeared into the back seat and emerged a few seconds later with a few six packs of beer. Her eyebrows wiggled as she nodded.

I chuckled as I followed after her. We didn't need to search the beach for Archer. By the time we got back, he had a roaring fire set up where we'd left him. I could see his face as he stood next to the flames, watching them. The light bounced around his features as he stared into it.

"Drink?" Clementine asked as she pulled one off and tossed it toward him.

Archer didn't even have to look as he reached out and caught the can. Clementine set up her phone to play music, and the sound filled the silence. I found a spot on the sand and brought my knees up to rest my chin on them.

I felt so calm. So…at home. Which wasn't something I'd ever felt before. Every place I'd lived had been just a placeholder for me. Even at Dad's house, I'd never felt like that was the place I was meant to be.

Every home I'd lived in, my parents', Dad's, even Sean's, had been the home I'd gone to for someone else. It had never been just…mine.

But here in Magnolia, I felt free for the first time. The inn, the one that was run-down and dusty, was mine. It was a place I'd chosen to go for myself. Having Clementine and Archer here helped solidify the fact that I was where I needed to be.

It felt as if Magnolia had been waiting for me. And maybe it was because this was where Dorthy had been. For some reason, I felt a kinship to her, a woman I'd never met. Seeing her in that photo, surrounded by friends, caused an ache to grow inside of me.

It pulled at a desire that I hadn't even known existed. That I'd spent my whole life ignoring. The desire for a sisterhood. A group of women to call my friends.

"Ah," Clementine sighed as she plopped down next to me. She looked deliriously happy as she sipped on her beer. "You don't want one?" she asked as she shook the can in my direction.

"Naw," I said as I reached out and grabbed a fistful of sand. "I need to be up bright and early tomorrow morning to work."

Clementine tsked me. "On an island, there's work time and then there's playtime." She shoved her finger into the sand as if she were trying to make a point. "This is playtime."

I chuckled and nodded but didn't take the beer she offered. "I'm good."

Clementine sighed as she took a sip. "So how do you like Magnolia so far?"

I couldn't help the smile that emerged. "I like it. A lot."

Clementine studied me for a moment before she turned her gaze out to the ocean. A sad expression drifted over her features as she stared hard at the water. "It's a good town, but it can feel like a cage sometimes. It can be a place where dreams go to die."

"Do you mean Juilliard?"

She turned to look at me. "Archer told you?"

I nodded. "Yeah."

She sighed as she took another sip. "I couldn't go. Dad needed me to stay."

I wrapped my arm around her shoulders and pulled her closer. "That's why you are an incredible person."

She nodded as she set her beer down and then wrapped her arms around her knees. I dropped my arm and did the same. An idea was floating around in my mind, and I figured now was the time to pass it by her.

"What do you think about starting up a book club?"

"A what?"

"A book club. Like in the photo we found."

Clementine studied me. "A book club," she repeated. Then she smiled. "What would we read?"

I shrugged. "I don't know. I'm sure we could find a list online or something. I just think it would be fun. You know, bring a little tradition back to the inn." I peeked over at her to see her staring into the fire. She looked contemplative as she rubbed her arm with her hand.

"I think that sounds fun." She turned to face me. "I think that sounds like a lot of fun."

I smiled. "Perfect." Then I furrowed my brow. "Can you head up getting more people involved. More than just you and I?"

Clementine laughed. "Of course. That'll be my job. You work on getting the inn presentable. I'll take care of everything else."

Our conversation shifted to Clementine's plans for tomorrow. She was disappointed to have to go back to work. I extended my arms behind me and leaned back. It was nice, just sitting there not worrying about what to say. Clementine was content with talking, and I was content with listening.

My gaze wandered over to Archer. He was next to the fire with his elbow behind him. He was picking at the sand.

I wondered what he was thinking about. Could he hear Clementine? Or was he thinking about his daughter? About his wife? The memory of his hug felt as fresh as the day it happened.

There was so much about Archer that I wanted to know, and yet, I wasn't sure how to ask. It wasn't my place just to bring stuff up, but on the other hand, he wasn't exactly pushing me away.

Maybe he was waiting for an opening, and I needed to be the one to give it to him.

"Hold on," Clementine suddenly said, drawing my attention over to her.

I raised my eyebrows. "What?"

Clementine's lips were parted and were making an "o" shape. "If we're called The Red Stiletto Book Club, does that mean we need to wear red stilettos?"

I shrugged. "It wouldn't be a necessity, but it could be fun."

Clementine slowly began to smile. "Oh, I think it should be a requirement. Bring a little class to the ladies of Magnolia."

I laughed and nodded. "Sounds good. We can make it a requirement."

Clementine clapped her hands and let out a laugh. "I'm so excited."

We spent the next hour hanging out by the fire. The warmth helped against the cool sea air. Without the sun, the temperature dropped. Maybe it was my exhaustion or the fact that I was sitting outside in shorts and a t-shirt, but I had to hug my legs to my chest to keep warm.

Clementine was lying in the sand with her eyes closed. Archer stood, and I watched as he started walking toward the ocean. Curiosity—and maybe the desire to walk next to him—won out, so I stood and followed.

Not sure what to do, I decided to just talk. What harm could come from that?

"Thanks," I said as I finally fell into step with him.

Archer paused and then glanced down at me. "For what?" he asked. Thankfully, he slowed his step, which gave me the confidence to keep talking. After all, he could easily quicken his pace and leave me in the dust.

The idea that he might actually want to talk to me made me giddy. In a ridiculous way.

"For helping me with the inn," I said. The waves lapped at my feet as I walked. The water was cool and refreshing.

"You are paying me," Archer started and then stopped and turned to face me. "You *are* paying me, right?"

I laughed as I glanced over at him. His gaze was teasing as he met mine. "Of course." Mom had given her skeptical approval in her last email. I told her how hard of a worker Archer was, so she'd reluctantly agreed to hire him on.

He chuckled. "Good." Then he continued down the beach. "How do you like Magnolia?" he asked.

I was grateful for his question. It meant I wasn't annoying him. If he wanted me gone, he'd just ignore me.

"Well, I haven't seen much of it, but from what I can tell, it's a lovely place. The people are nice. The scenery is superb." I reached down and picked up a seashell. "Much better than New York."

He nodded. "Yeah. When I was at Yale, I missed it here. Collette—" My gaze snapped up to see him pinch his lips together at the mention of his ex-wife. He paused before he sighed. "My ex-wife hated living in a small town. She wasn't too thrilled when I asked if we could move back here. If I'd known what would happen with Elise, I never would have pushed for it either." His voice drifted off, and I watched as his gaze dropped to the ground.

Not wanting him to feel alone, I took in a deep breath. "Sean never wanted to live anywhere but New York." I felt Archer's gaze on me, but I continued anyway. "My ex-husband had a thing for the city...and apparently my friend." I offered him a small smile. I wanted to show him that he could trust me. That I understood what it was like to be disappointed in love. In life.

"You were married?" he asked.

"Yep. For ten years." I sighed as I chucked the seashell into the ocean. "He wasn't good for me, but I didn't see that until he'd dragged me so far down, it was hard to see the light anymore." I peeked over at Archer to see him studying me. "Good riddance, right?"

Archer's jaw muscles tightened as he nodded. "Yeah."

"That's why being here is so great." I paused as the ocean breeze picked up and wrapped me inside of it. I closed my eyes as took in a deep, cleansing breath. "This is the first thing I've done for myself in a long time," I said, my voice coming out with reverence.

There was a sense of self-love that was starting to sprout inside of me. Maybe it was Magnolia. Maybe it was the sense of accomplishment that working on this inn gave me.

Whatever it was, I could get used to this new Maggie. She was someone I wanted to get to know. When I finally peeked over at Archer, my heart began to pound inside of my chest.

From the look in his eye and the softness of his expression, a ridiculous thought passed through my mind.

One that told me this Maggie was someone he wanted to get to know as well.

12

CLEMENTINE

I was a woman on a mission.

Sitting at the counter at the hardware store the next day, I stared at the invitation I'd just created on my computer. It was for the book club that Maggie wanted to start.

After I got home last night, the book club was all I could think about. It felt amazing to think about something other than wrenches or screwdrivers or Dad. It was the first thing I'd been excited about in a long time, and I was ready to get it underway.

I stared at the font I'd picked and shook my head. I selected the text and moved to find something more pleasing. Just as I did, the door chimed, and I glanced up to see Shari walk in. Her eyes looked red and puffy. Her hair was disheveled, and I could tell she hadn't slept.

I closed my computer and slipped off the stool. "Hey," I

said as I rounded the counter and wrapped my arm around her shoulder. "What's wrong?"

She sniffled and shrugged as she swiped at her eyes. "Allergies," she murmured. "That mixed with Tag throwing up all night, and I'm exhausted." She wandered over to the small-appliance section of the store and squatted down.

"Shar," I said as I grabbed her arm and pulled her up. I guided her over to the chair I'd just vacated and pushed on her shoulders until she sat. She hesitated at first, but she finally relented and settled down.

I hurried into the break room, where I grabbed a cup of coffee and a doughnut from the box that Spencer had brought in earlier. With both in hand, I made my way to the front and dropped the food onto the counter in front of my friend.

Shari stared at them for a moment before she picked both up and began to devour the doughnut in between sips of coffee. I folded my arms as I rested them on the countertop and leaned forward. "Now, tell me what you are looking for, and I'll get it for you."

Shari blew out her breath and nodded. "A dehumidifier. Tag's room is musty, and I'm worried it's because it's too humid in there."

I gave her a resolute nod and went to grab one. When I got back, Shari had finished her doughnut and was sipping slowly on the coffee. She looked a little more alive than she had when she first walked in.

Not wanting her to leave before we could talk, I

pushed the box to the side and focused my attention on her. "Where's Craig?" I asked as I folded my arms.

She wouldn't meet my gaze as she fiddled with the handle of her mug. Anger rose up inside of me, but I pushed it down. I didn't want to make her upset, but I also didn't want her to think I agreed with how she was handling things.

It was a tricky situation. On the one hand, we were friends. She was probably the closest friend I had on the island. But I knew she was keeping things from me. How close can two people be when one of them is keeping secrets?

I pushed those thoughts from my head as I focused back on Shari. No matter what was happening, I wanted to be there for her. And I would. "Check this out," I said as I opened my computer and showed her the invitation.

"Red Stiletto Book Club? What's that?" she asked.

I smiled. "Apparently, it's a book club that used to meet over at Magnolia Inn. Maggie's wanting to start it up again. Figured it would be a way to get the ladies here to meet and spend time together. Plus, her grandmother used to head it up."

Shari smiled as she glanced over at me. "I think that it's a great idea. Want me to pass some out at the school? I'm sure there are some teachers who are dying for cheese and wine," she said as she tapped her finger on the part of the invitation where I'd included that info.

I nodded. "Maybe after a few goes. Maggie's wanting to keep it small for now." I pressed print and walked into my office to grab the fliers off the printer. "I want you there though," I said as I handed her an invitation.

Shari nodded and slipped it into her purse. "Awesome. I'll be there." She pulled shut the zipper on her purse and blew out her breath. "I should get going. Cathy is watching Tag, but she could only do it for an hour, and I have another place I have to stop by before I head back."

I smiled and nodded as Shari climbed off the stool and walked toward the front door.

"I'll see you later?" she asked.

I waved at her as the door slid shut.

"A book club?"

I screamed and turned to see Victoria standing there with her arms crossed and her eyebrows raised. She ran her gaze over me as she tapped her fingers on her forearms.

"Eavesdrop much?" I asked as I moved to slip the invitations onto a back shelf and out of view. "I'm not sure what you're talking about." I gave her the widest, fakest smile I could muster.

Victoria sighed as she took a step forward. "I heard you talking to Shari. Why are you making this weird?"

I sighed as my shoulders slumped. Victoria and I had a sketchy past. We grew up together. Went to the same schools. There was a stint of time where she crushed on Archer. She was aggressive and snobby and not someone I wanted to spend my time with.

Or invite to our book club.

But she was standing there. And she had heard our

conversation. There really wasn't a way I could play this off. I had no other choice but to invite her. If I didn't want her making my life miserable for the next five years.

I leaned down and grabbed an invite. "Here," I said.

Victoria took it, and after a quick scan, she folded it in half and stuffed it into her purse. "I'll come, and I approve."

I furrowed my brow. "Why would we need—"

"I actually think it's a great idea. Great for my reelection campaign. I'm trying to have more community involvement," Victoria interrupted. Her father was a senator of Rhode Island. Politics were bred into her family, and Victoria took that legacy seriously. There was nothing she wouldn't do to maintain her status.

I forced a smile. "Wonderful," I said through my clenched teeth. The last thing I wanted to do was help Victoria with anything, but I'd gone this far. It wasn't like I could pull the invite out of her purse and proclaim that it was all a joke.

Victoria nodded as she pushed the boxes of lightbulbs she'd set down on the counter toward me. "I'll take these," she said.

I rang her up, she paid, and a minute later, she left.

I blew out my breath as I collapsed on the stool behind me, allowing my arms to hang down at my sides. Victoria made me tense, and now this fun event I was hosting with Maggie had changed.

Refusing to let Victoria rain on my parade anymore, I cleared my throat and stood. I had shelves to restock. I had enough work to keep me busy from now until Michelle got here to run the evening shift.

After a quick check-in with Dad, I got busy.

By the time Michelle arrived, I was sweaty and tired and ready to get out of the store. Dad had eaten dinner and was now relaxing in his bed, and I doubted he'd get out for anything. I nodded toward Michelle, who took up residence behind the register. Once I'd changed and grabbed my purse, I headed back downstairs, where I grabbed the stack of invitations. I handed one to Michelle and headed out the door.

I was going to stop by the diner first and then head over to Shakes. After handing a few fliers out, I wandered over to The Hideout coffee shop and pulled open the door. The smell of java and cream filled my nose as the espresso machine let out its familiar hiss.

Anna was standing behind the counter. Her greying hair was pulled back into a bun, and she wore a coffee-splotched apron over a grey t-shirt. When she looked up, she smiled. "Well, good evening, Clem," she said.

Anna and my mother had been friends for a long time. Well, I'd be hard pressed to find someone on the island that my mom hadn't been friends with. When Mom passed away, Anna had taken on a sort of mothering role for Archer and me.

"Hey," I said as I leaned against the counter. I reached out and grabbed one of the chocolate chip cookie samples she had in small paper cups. I munched on it as I surveyed the board of drinks. After I ordered, I stepped off to the side.

"How are things at the store?" she asked. "Dirk doing well?"

I shrugged as I unwrapped the cookie I'd just bought. "Same old, same old. Dad's doing well. He hasn't had too many outbursts, which is nice. He loves his schedule."

Anna nodded as she finished making my iced Americano. Once she snapped the lid on, she handed it over to me. I grabbed a straw and pulled the paper off.

"That's good to hear."

I nodded as I took a sip.

"Anything else going on in your life?"

I nodded as I pulled out an invitation for the book club and handed it to her. She took it, and as her gaze swept over the paper, a small smile spread across her lips.

"I haven't seen that name in a long time," she said with reverence.

I furrowed my brow. "The Red Stiletto Book Club?" I asked.

Anna nodded as she ran her fingers across the words. "I was part of it for a short time." Her expression got a far-off look in it. "Dorthy really knew how to throw a party."

I laughed. "And read a book?"

Anna folded her arms. "A book club is so much more than just a group of ladies reading the same book. There's a sort of sisterhood that comes out of it. A bond that can't be replicated anywhere else." She handed the piece of paper back to me. "You'll love it."

I took it and slipped it back into my purse with the others. "I'm excited for it to start."

Anna tapped her fingers on the counter as she studied me. I met her gaze. "What's up?" I asked. I could see she wanted to ask me something.

"I'm not sure if you've heard or not, but my daughter and grandson are moving in with me."

I shook my head. "Fiona's coming back?"

Fiona was Anna's twenty-five-year-old daughter who moved to Knoxville when she was nineteen. She had chased some guy who claimed he was destined to be a big country singer. Things didn't go so well, and he left her with a baby and no job.

Anna nodded. "Yes. I finally convinced her to come home."

"That's good."

Anna blew out her breath and gave me a look that said, *you have no idea.* "I was wondering if I could give her one of those invitations. It might be good for her, connecting with others her age here in Magnolia. She's having a hard time coming to grips with returning, and this might soften the blow."

I retrieved the invitation she'd given back to me. "Of course. We'd love to have her come."

Anna took the piece of paper, folded it, and set it reverently next to the register. "You're so sweet, Clem. I know she really looked up to you growing up, and being invited will mean a lot."

I shrugged as I finished the last bite of my cookie and

washed it down with my drink. "Anything I can do to help."

Anna shot me a smile and then turned to help Ben Williams who had approached the register. I walked past him, getting a huge whiff of fish as I did. Ben had a habit of fishing off the dock at Magnolia beach. He went out every day and cast his line.

He was a good-looking guy, if only he'd cut his hair and beard. He was three years younger than me, but with his fishing hat and tan vest, he looked twenty years older.

An ache I hadn't felt for a long time rose up inside of me. His look. That smell. All of it reminded me of Jake.

I muscled down those feelings. Thinking about Jake—feeling anything for him—wasn't allowed.

He was gone, and I'd moved on.

Sort of.

The next hour passed quickly, and once I had handed out the last of the invitations, I headed home. I was exhausted and ready for a shower and some dinner. By the time I walked into the apartment, it was dark and the only light came from the over-the-sink light in the kitchen and from the cracks around Archer's closed door.

I thought about knocking to see how the day had gone at Maggie's but decided against it. Instead, I made myself a quick sandwich and poured a glass of wine, and then I headed to the bathroom where I started the bath.

After soaking for an hour, I got out and dried off.

I dressed in my pajamas and crawled into bed, exhaustion taking over my body. Before I fell asleep, I grabbed my phone and texted Maggie.

Handed out the invitations. Everyone seems excited about it! I've got to work tomorrow, but maybe we can go for dinner?

I waited for a response with my eyes closed and my comforter pulled up to my chin. A few seconds later, my phone chimed.

Perfect, and yes, let's do dinner tomorrow.

With that response, I turned my phone to silent and closed my eyes. Even though I felt too excited to sleep, I was finally able to quiet my mind and relax my body enough so that darkness took over and I fell asleep.

13

MAGGIE

A week later, I woke up to the sun streaming into my room. I squeezed my eyes shut and made a mental note to buy drapes this afternoon. One of the great things about the internet was that everything was at my fingertips. On an island with limited shopping options, that was a must.

Realizing that sleep was going to evade me, I pulled my covers off and padded over to my bathroom. This last week, Archer and a few guys on the island had been making their rounds in the bathrooms, fixing them up, and making sure they worked.

They supported my desire to keep the original charm, so they did very little demolition—unless there was unrecoverable damage. They took care to protect the current tile and fixtures while they worked, which I was grateful for.

The inn was slowly coming together thanks to Archer and his friends.

I turned on the shower and waited for the water to warm up. The inn's progress had me feeling more bummed than excited. The more Archer got done around here, the more the moment I would have to sell came to the forefront of my mind.

Thankfully, Penny had stepped back and let me do what I wanted. She texted a few times, asking for some progress photos, but that was about all the contact we had. I appreciated the fact that she was more hands-off. It gave me the freedom to do what I felt was right for the place.

After I showered, I wrapped my hair up in a towel and dressed in a pair of cutoff shorts and a black tank. I was in the process of tackling the living room, wiping down the walls and the floor in preparation for the sander that was scheduled to be dropped off today.

After pricing out floor restorers, I discovered I could save quite a bit if I just did them myself. I watched countless videos about how to do it, and I felt pretty confident that I could handle this task. Plus, with Archer here, that confidence only grew.

Now dressed, I opened my door and padded out to the kitchen, where I filled the coffee pot and started the machine. It hummed to life as I pulled out eggs and bread. I busied myself with making breakfast as the smell of freshly brewed coffee filled the air.

Just as I cracked the last egg in the pan, my phone rang.

I glanced over to my screen to see *Penny* flash on the screen. My heart took off galloping as I wiped my fingers on the nearby towel and hit talk. I pinched the phone between my shoulder and ear. "Hello?"

"Margaret?"

I gulped. "Hey, Penny."

There was a sigh on the other end. I furrowed my brow as I pushed the eggs around the pan with a spatula. Why did she have that reaction? She was the one who called me.

A few seconds ticked by, and just when I started to fear that I'd accidentally hung up on her, she continued, "How is restoration going?"

I nodded. "Good. Things are coming along. Did you get the pictures I emailed to you?"

"Yes. I did. I can see the change. Things are looking good."

I blinked a few times. Did my mother just compliment me? "Thanks?" I asked, still not sure how to take what she'd said.

More silence. I began to grow uncomfortable with our conversation. I felt like a child waiting to get scolded, and I hated that. After all, if she was upset with something, she should come out and tell me.

"I'm calling to let you know I plan on dropping by next week."

My entire body froze. "Drop by?" This was Rhode Island we were talking about. It wasn't just an hour drive.

It was going to take a plane ride for her to get here. Why would she classify her trip so casually?

"Fly in, actually. I will send you my flight information, so keep an eye out for that." Then she cleared her throat. "I'm interested to see the progress with my own eyes."

I nodded, still speechless from her announcement. Then, realizing that she couldn't see me, I cleared my throat and managed, "We'll be ready."

Penny said a formal goodbye and hung up.

I remained standing in front of the stove with my eggs popping and my phone still sandwiched in the crook of my neck. My mind was swirling from what Penny had said.

She was coming here? Next week?

My heart picked up speed. The inn was nowhere near ready to be seen by her. If she was coming, that meant I needed to get to work.

Now.

"Are you okay?"

I screamed and turned to see Archer peering down at me. My heart was pounding as the shock of seeing him plus Penny's phone call coursed through me. I straightened, which caused my phone to slip off my shoulder. Just before it crashed to the ground, Archer moved to catch it.

"Whoa," he said as he set it on the counter next to the stove. Then he turned his attention back to me. "Are you okay? You look like you saw a ghost."

I tried to focus my thoughts as I murmured, "Penny. A ghost. Pretty much the same thing."

Archer furrowed his brow. "Who's Penny?"

Not wanting my eggs to turn rubbery or worse, burn, I focused my attention back on the pan. Archer didn't hesitate. He found a plate and held it out for me to scrape the eggs onto.

I was grateful for his foresight. With the way my mind was reeling, I couldn't really process anything.

With my eggs and a cup of coffee in hand, I wandered over to the small card table that Clementine had brought over for me to use. Clem and I had spent the last few nights together, either here or at one of the restaurants in town. We'd even gone to see a movie last weekend.

It was nice to have someone to hang out with. She helped me feel less alone in this big house. Plus, I was beginning to really enjoy spending time with Archer. When he smiled at me, I got the feeling that he liked spending time with me, too.

There had been a few moments this last week that I thought, maybe, he liked me more than in the *you're my boss and my little sister's friend* way, but I instantly pushed that thought from my mind. After all, the last thing I needed to do was act on any of those hints that I thought I was picking up.

I didn't want to ruin one of the two relationships I'd really cultivated here in Magnolia.

Archer sat down across from me and sighed. He stretched back on the chair as his gaze wandered around the room. It was nice, the fact that I was beginning to feel more and more relaxed in his presence.

"It's really coming along," he said with a hint of reverence in his voice that sent shivers down my back.

I pinched my lips together as I nodded. Focusing on eating seemed the best option for me.

When I didn't answer, his gaze drifted to me, and he furrowed his brow. "You okay?" he asked.

I took a sip of my coffee, and after a moment, I shook my head. "I got a call from my mom."

Archer leaned forward and rested his forearms on the table. "And that's a bad thing?"

I nodded. "If you knew my mother, you would agree."

"She's coming?"

I eyed him. "Yes."

He chuckled. "Then I'll get to meet her."

I narrowed my eyes in a playful manner. "You'll regret it." I scooped up the last of my eggs and shoveled them into my mouth.

Archer let out a *pish* sound as he leaned back on the chair once more. "The woman who created you? I doubt that."

Heat pricked at my skin as my gaze snapped to Archer. He didn't seem to mind the words that just left his lips. Instead, he'd dropped his focus down to his hands, which were resting in his lap, and took in a deep breath as if complimenting the woman in front of him was an everyday occurrence.

I blinked a few times, trying to figure out if he'd said what I thought he'd said. Was it a compliment? Was he flirting?

I wanted to bury my head in my hands. Scratch that. I wanted a hole to open up in the floor and swallow me whole. I didn't want to interpret his words as anything other than something one friend would say to another— but I couldn't help it.

I was beginning to like Archer. More than just as a friend. He was sweet and kind, and despite the fact that he kept to himself, the moments when he opened up and let me in made my heart sing. Loud and off key.

I decided to brush off his comment with something real. It seemed appropriate in the moment. He was lowering his guard. I could to the same.

"There are moments I doubt I even came from the woman," I said softly. It hurt how true those words felt.

Archer glanced up at me with his brow furrowed. "Why?"

I twisted my mug on the table as I filtered through my thoughts. There was a lot I wanted to tell Archer but also didn't want to bombard him with my problems. "She's just different than me. She's poised and elegant. Everything she does succeeds. Everything she touches turns to gold."

I cleared my throat as my emotions rose up inside of it. I hated that even talking about her could elicit a feeling like this. I needed to be stronger. I'd spent my whole life proclaiming that I was okay. That her words of disappointment or the way she looked at me didn't really matter.

That I was enough for myself and that was all that mattered.

Except, that was a lie that I was struggling to tell myself. Especially since every person who should love me seemed to think that I wasn't enough.

Sean. Penny. They couldn't see how desperately I wanted to be accepted as just me. Plain old, nothing special, me.

I sighed and stood as I gathered my dishes and walked over to the sink; then I rinsed them and stacked them in the dishwasher. Once the kitchen was clean, I dried my hands on the nearby hand towel and turned to see Archer had gotten up from the table and was now leaning against the counter with his legs extended and his arm folded across his chest.

His eyes were narrowed as he studied me. I swallowed and then smiled at him. What was he thinking? I did take a small amount of pleasure in the fact that he felt comfortable enough with me that he wasn't dropping his gaze and avoiding talking to me—like he'd done the first few times we met.

Our relationship had definitely deepened through working together.

Archer cleared his throat and stood as he waved toward my room. "Get ready. We're going across the bridge."

I raised my eyebrows. "We are?"

He nodded. "I have to pick up some tile, and you need to get out of the house." He stepped closer to me. "I'm going to take you to see the beauty of Magnolia."

His movement had brought his body close to me. Even though we weren't touching, I could feel his warmth wash over me. I fought the urge to close my eyes and take in a deep breath. The small hints of his cologne that were currently surrounding me were making my senses go haywire.

I wanted to lean in. I wanted to take in more of him. For a moment, I allowed myself to wonder what it would be like to be touched by him. To feel his arms around me.

It had been so long since I'd been touched by a man, that I was beginning to fade ever so slightly. There were studies done on touching. A person couldn't survive if they weren't touched on a regular basis.

With Sean, he'd rarely touched me, and when he did, it was for his enjoyment, not mine. But when Archer looked at me, when he leaned into me, suddenly my history with men meant nothing. I got the inkling that I had no idea what it was to be touched by a man. To be loved by one.

One look at Archer, and I didn't need to have it confirmed any other way. Archer knew how to hold a woman. He knew what to do.

My heart pounded so hard that I could hear my pulse in my ears. I held my breath as I raised my gaze to study him. To take him in.

"Is that okay?" he asked. The tone of his voice had deepened, and the intensity of his gaze took my breath away.

"Sure," I said quietly.

He studied me for a moment longer before he nodded and stepped back, pulling his handyman belt off and setting it on the counter.

"I'll be right back," I said as I turned and hurried to my room. Even though my mind was reeling—I really should stay and work, especially with the threat of Penny's visit looming over me—I decided, for this one day, I'd ignore it.

I had not stopped working since I got here, and I was ready to let my hair down and spend some time getting to know Magnolia—and, in the quiet part of my mind, Archer.

I changed into a flowy, white summer dress with strappy sandals. I pulled my hair down and ran a comb through it. I applied a little makeup—not enough to look like I was trying, but enough to make me look somewhat attractive. Then I shouldered my purse, took in a deep breath, and headed out the door.

Archer was standing in the kitchen when I returned. A few of the guys he'd hired were standing around him as Archer gave them instructions for things to do while we were gone.

Apparently, the kitchen was next on the list. The guys were to install the appliances that had been delivered earlier this week after they replaced the yellowing linoleum with tile that looked like hardwood. Then they were to work on the cupboards, sanding and re-staining them to their oaken glory.

I stood off to the side as I watched Archer talk. His eyes were so full of life compared to when I first met him.

He looked at peace, instructing these men. I could tell he was a man who was meant to lead. It made me sad that fate had decided to turn its back on him as well.

Archer must have sensed my gaze because, a moment later, he glanced over at me. He didn't break our connection as he smiled at me. It wasn't until Tom, his second-in-command, spoke that he glanced over.

A shiver ran up my back as I slowly blew out my breath. His stare had warmed a part of me that I thought had died a long time ago. Back when Sean would tell me how unworthy I was of anything. That my life didn't matter as much as his did.

After all, he was the breadwinner. It was my job to let myself fail so he could succeed. I'd spent so many nights believing that what Sean said was true. That I wasn't meant to accomplish anything.

But being with Archer made me feel like everything I'd been told was wrong. It was like he saw me for who I was deep down. That Maggie Brown was worth it. Whatever I wanted, I deserved it.

Not wanting to embarrass myself in front of Archer by crying or having my cheeks turn bright red, I turned my body so that I could take in a few cleansing breaths. I needed to get a hold of my emotions before I broke down.

That would put a damper on our fun, relaxing outing.

"Ready?" Archer's voice was low, and all my efforts to control my body temperature and breathing went right out the window when I realized just how close he was behind me.

I could feel his warmth. I could sense him in every part of my being. He was a breath away from me, and he wasn't moving. Instead, he stayed, standing next to me.

I pinched my lips together and nodded as I took a few steps forward. As much as I loved having him close, there was still a part of me that sent off warning bells at his proximity. The part of me that reminded me that, in my history with men, they always hurt me.

That I was never going to be good enough for Archer.

Besides, even if I believed that Archer and I were possible, it didn't change the fact that my time on the island was temporary. I was here to fix the inn and then leave.

Archer had already said goodbye to too many people. I couldn't ask him to do that with me.

Without missing a beat, Archer reached out and rested his hand on my lower back. Warmth exploded through me as he guided me through the inn and out the front door. When we got to his truck, he jogged to the passenger side, opened the door, and waited for me to approach.

I climbed in and buckled my seatbelt. Once I was situated, he shut the door and then rounded the hood. He jumped in the driver's seat and started the engine. Just before he pulled out, he shot me another heartwarming smile.

"Ready?" he asked as if he'd proposed something more exciting than going to pick up tiles. He had a teasing hint in his voice and a flirty gaze that I couldn't ignore.

I swallowed and nodded. "Yes," I whispered.

Archer let out a chuckle as his hand brushed my shoulder. He'd stretched out his arm so he could glance over his shoulder as he pulled out of the parking lot. Then he settled back as he turned onto the main road and we drove off.

14

MAGGIE

T he feel of the warm breeze on my arm as
Archer drove down the road that hugged the
beach in Magnolia felt like heaven on my skin.
My window was rolled down, and I was moving my hand
up and down in the air, reveling in the feeling of air as it
rushed across my body.

Archer had his aviator sunglasses on, and Johnny Cash
sang from his speakers. His shoulders were relaxed. His
wrist was resting on the steering wheel. The road curved
and rose along with the scenery as if the person who
created it had taken great pains to keep the integrity of the
landscape rather than slice through it.

The first thing on Archer's must-do-in-Magnolia list
was drive along the coastline. Since this was an island—
and a small one at that—he promised it wouldn't take
long. I just needed to see what Magnolia had to offer.

I wanted to tell him that just by looking in his direction, I'd already seen everything that I wanted to see—but I kept that to myself. Having thoughts like that scared me, and I was pretty sure that declaring those thoughts out loud would scare him too.

I felt Archer's gaze on me, so I turned to meet it. He had a suspicious smile on his lips as he pulled off to the side of the road and into a small gravel parking lot. Off in the distance, I saw a small lighthouse. I raised my eyebrows as I glanced back at him.

"Gelato," he said. On his side of the truck was a small, one-room shack. There were a few picnic tables scattered about under umbrellas. I pulled open my door and stepped out into the warm sunlight. I inhaled as I stretched and then rounded the hood to find Archer waiting for me.

He had his hands tucked into his front pockets, and he was leaning against the truck. When he saw me, he straightened and nodded toward the shack's small window with a ledge that extended out like a makeshift ordering counter.

"Gelato?" I asked as I fell into step with him.

He nodded. "You can't live on Magnolia and not know about Mama Schmidt's Gelato."

"Mama Schmidt?" I asked.

Archer gave me a side smile as he approached the window and knocked solidly on the glass. I waited as the sound of something dropping in the back filled the air. I peered inside to see a younger woman—well, younger than the name Mama Schmidt conjured up for me—round the corner and run her gaze over us.

"Archer?" she asked as she pushed her red curly hair from her face. "It's been a while," she said as she turned on the faucet and washed her hands.

"It has been a while, Scar. I was happy to hear when you opened for the season," Archer said as he leaned his shoulder against the glass and smiled at her.

A ridiculous twinge of jealousy rose up inside of me as I witnessed their interaction. Even though the glass of the window was cloudy, I could see that her cheeks were pink. And the way she kept glancing up at Archer and then back down told me there was history here.

"What can I get you?" she asked.

Archer turned his attention to me and extended his hand. As if Scar finally noticed that I was there, she turned her gaze to me.

"Hi," I said. I moved to extend my hand but then felt ridiculous when I realized that there was no way she could shake it. So I quickly dropped it. "What's good here?" I asked as I threaded my hand around the strap of my purse as if it were my lifeline.

"Everything," Scar said.

"I get the black cherry gelato. It's the best." Archer's voice was suddenly very close.

I turned to see that his face was inches from mine. I had the thought of pulling back, but something inside of me—a ridiculous part of me that wanted to show Scar that

Archer just might like me—forced me to stay put. And smile. Widely.

"It's good?" I asked.

Archer smiled. "It's to die for."

I nodded and then turned back to Scar. "I'd love a serving of that, then."

Scar nodded. "Same for you, Arch?"

He nodded, and before I could fish any money out of my purse, he slipped a twenty into the little opening under the window. Scar took it, and as she turned to the register to get his change, Archer waved her away.

"Keep the change. Consider it payment for the bill to clean out your car." I wasn't sure, but from the way his left cheek crinkled, I swear he winked at Scar.

When I glanced back at her, I saw that her cheeks were red again and she was laughing. "That was years ago. I would have completely forgotten about it if you hadn't brought it up."

Archer shrugged. "I always pay my debts, even if they are decades late."

Scar nodded, tucked the twenty into the drawer, and then disappeared through the doorway.

Not sure how to interpret anything that I'd just witnessed, I turned to face Archer. How did I ask the burning questions I had inside? Who was Scar? Were they dating? It didn't seem like they were, but they clearly weren't strangers.

Archer must have sensed my curiosity because a

moment later, he said, "We've known each other since high school."

I smiled and nodded, hating that he felt like he needed to justify his actions to me. Who was I to him besides his boss? He could date or talk to whomever he wanted. He didn't need to tell me.

"Oh, that's nice," I said as I reached out and pulled a few napkins from the dispenser next to the window.

"Her grandmother started Mama Schmidt's Gelato," he offered.

I glanced up at him and smiled. I wasn't sure why he kept going on. He had a history. So did I. "Oh," I said.

Archer narrowed his eyes. "At a senior party, I threw up in the back of her car. Had a little too much to drink," he said again.

I nodded. "I figured."

A few seconds ticked by, and then the side door of the shack opened as Scar brought out our gelato. She and Archer chatted for a few more minutes.

She even talked to me. I told her I was fixing up Magnolia Inn. She told me her name was Scarlet and that she'd love to come see the inn. Apparently, her grandmother and Dorthy had been friends as well.

It was nice talking to her. So much so that I invited her to join the book club. She said she didn't have much time for reading—apparently her other side hustle was fishing —but that she'd try to make it. I left my number with her and told her I'd text her with more information as Archer took his gelato and headed toward the lighthouse.

I gave her a quick wave and headed after Archer. We walked in silence once I fell into step with him. The ground had turned rocky, and I made sure to watch where I placed my feet. The last thing I needed was to slip and fall on my butt in front of Archer.

Talk about humiliation.

"So, you're going to start up this book club?" Archer asked once we got to the lighthouse. It was windy, causing my hair to dance around my face. I tried my best to tuck it behind my ear, and for the most part, it worked.

"Yeah," I said as I scooped up the gelato and slipped it into my mouth. The creamy, smooth texture was like heaven on my tongue. That mixed with the tartness of the cherries had my taste buds singing.

"That's exciting," he said as he kept his gaze out toward the ocean. "I like that you are making plans to stay longer."

I blew out my breath and nodded. "It's strange. Even though I've never met my grandmother, it's almost as if starting this club is a way for me to get close to her."

I felt Archer's gaze on me, and for a moment, I refused to look at him. There was an intensity in his stare that I could feel. It was as if he was looking, *really* looking, at me.

My heart pounded, and that reaction scared me.

A lot.

"Clem and I are adopted. Did she tell you that?"

I glanced over at him and nodded. She'd told me in one of our evening conversations.

Archer gave me a soft smile. "I get your desire to

connect with your family. As much as I love my adoptive parents, it's hard to not want to know more." He finished his gelato, set his bowl down, and picked up a rock. He threw it up in the air and caught it a few times before turning his attention to the ocean.

"You were a lawyer?" I blurted out. Pinching my lips together, my cheeks heated when I realized what I'd just asked. I'm sure Archer didn't want me to know about his past, and for me to just bring it up so casually felt like an invasion of his privacy.

Archer paused before he looked over his shoulder. "Clem tell you about me?"

I cleared my throat and decided to focus on shoveling the last bits of gelato into my mouth. Anything to distract myself from asking any more prying questions.

"She told you about me," he said a couple seconds later. It was apparent that he knew his sister all too well.

"Just that," I whispered. I didn't want him to think I'd been prying into his life. We were jiving so well, and I didn't want to scare him off in any way.

Archer glanced over at me, his eyes squinting. The sun was high in the sky now. Its warmth cascading over me. He studied me for a moment before his lips tipped up into a smile. "It's okay. We do live in Magnolia—the place where secrets are never kept. If it wasn't Clem, it would have been someone else."

I wrapped my arms around my chest and squeezed as I looked out toward the ocean. The breeze mixed with the warmth of the day surrounded me and made me feel at peace.

"My parents divorced when I was eight. It was hard, picking who to live with. My dad was the easy choice, and I've always wondered if my mom held my decision against me." I kept my gaze on the waves as they lapped at the shore.

From the corner of my eye, I saw Archer study me for a moment before he reached down and picked up another rock.

I took in a deep breath and continued. "Penny Brown is a determined, distant mother. I guess I just wished that she cared as much about her daughter as she did her success." I peeked over at Archer and hurried to add, "She's an editor in New York."

Archer held my gaze as he threw the rock up into the air a few times. Then he turned and threw it into the ocean. "I bet she cares more about you than she lets on."

I sighed and tightened my grip around my chest. "I don't know. I'm pretty much a failure in her book. My body, my job, my divorce. It's like all of those things are a stain on her reputation."

"Your body?"

Archer's question caught me off guard. Had I said that? I pinched my lips together as I ran my comment through my mind. Embarrassment coursed through me when I realized, yes, I had in fact said that.

"Why would your body be a failure?" As if to emphasize his question, he took a step back and ran his gaze over me.

I got the sudden urge to run away. To hide from his gaze. Did I want him looking at me like that? I guess I was okay with my figure when I thought no one was taking notice. But to have a man—an attractive man at that—step back and really look at me sent my insecurities into a panic.

"Because I look like this," I whispered as I watched Archer's lips tip up into a smile. It wasn't a mocking one. His smile, the light in his eyes, told me that he thought very differently about my body.

"If that's true, I'm pretty sure your mom is blind," he said as he turned his focus back to the ocean. "I'll never understand women. You think men want stick figures with nothing to hold onto. When in reality, it's the opposite."

I couldn't help but stare at him. Heat flushed my body as his voice deepened with his words. Part of me was questioning if he really said what he said or I'd been imagining it. It was as if he were speaking to every one of my insecurities. Sean always made me feel less than worthy for my cellulite and stretch marks. With what Archer just said, I was starting to wonder if he wouldn't mind.

I was mesmerized by the way his eyes narrowed. The way his jaw muscles flinched or his Adam's apple bobbed up and down with each swallow. It was mesmerizing to watch.

Then I realized that I was staring at him. Openly and

blatantly. Heat pricked my skin as I turned away from him. We stood there in silence for a few moments before he cleared his throat, bent down, and picked up his container. Then he reached out and grabbed my empty one. His fingers brushed mine as he did, sending an electrical current through my body at his touch.

My entire body tingled as he smiled down at me. "We should get going. We still have to go over the bridge," he said, his voice returning to a smooth cadence. He marked the end of his statement with a quick wink.

I nodded and followed after him.

We climbed into his truck, and soon we were back on the road. The trip over the bridge and into Newport took about thirty minutes. It was amazing how relaxed I felt around Archer. He had his window down and his elbow resting on the door.

Johnny Cash's deep, throaty voice filled the air. I settled back in my seat with my arms crossed and my gaze drifting to the world around us as Archer drove. The fresh spring air filled the cab of his truck. The smell of flowers and freshly cut grass permeated my senses.

I was disappointed when Archer pulled into the parking lot of a big chain hardware store and killed the engine. Intrigued about what he was getting, I climbed out and followed after him.

Once inside, I spent the next few hours shopping. Even though I wanted to keep the integrity of the inn, I still wanted some modern amenities. I knew once I switched out the shower heads, for example, the water pressure would increase. I also wanted to install ceiling fans in each room.

I even allowed myself to pick out a few rugs and some deck furniture. My excitement for the inn was building as I stood in the checkout line. Archer stepped up next to me with a box of tiles under his arm. He surveyed my purchases.

"I'm guessing it was a good thing we came, then," he said. There was a teasing hint to his voice that made me blush.

"Yeah, I'm kind of a nerd about these kinds of things."

He smiled as he began to load the boxes onto the checkout counter. We finished making our purchases, and I followed behind Archer as he rolled the cart from the store. I helped him load the back of the truck, and then we both climbed into the cab.

"If you liked that, I have a few other places to take you," he said as he started up the engine.

I couldn't help the smile that spread across my lips as I reached over and located my seatbelt. Once it was clicked in place, he pulled out of the parking spot and onto the main road.

Archer and I spent the rest of the afternoon shopping antique stores. He knew all the gem places, and when I walked into them, I was taken away. Every piece was handpicked and exquisite. My pulse quickened when I found wrought iron bed frames and pictures that took my breath away.

Thankfully, I had Archer there to lend me his critical

eye because I was ready to purchase the entire store. He helped reign me in and narrow down my selections to the must-haves.

As we walked out of the last store, I glanced up to see that the sun had begun to set. The air had cooled to a more manageable temperature, and the world around me seemed to slow. I thought I knew what happiness was, but standing here with my arms full of antique quilts and crocheted tablecloths, a feeling of warmth spread through every limb.

I'd never felt so at home or so at peace before. Living in New York didn't offer the sense of belonging like Rhode Island did. Everyone was kinder, gentler. They weren't worried about the next big thing. Instead, they lived in the moment.

The sound of the tailgate shutting drew my attention over. Archer dusted off his hands and then shoved them into the front pockets of his jeans. He leaned against the truck, and his gaze was focused on me.

He wasn't shy in his stare. I could feel his intensity as he studied me. His expression was raw and unabashed. When his gaze met mine, he smiled. I was beginning to grow accustomed to his smile. To the look in his gaze.

I returned his expression as I walked over to him. He straightened and gently took my items from me. As he placed them in the back of the cab, I stood nearby, watching him. I didn't move when he stepped back and slammed the door even though he was now standing inches away from me.

I was happy for the first time in a long time, and there was a part of me that knew part of that happiness came from Archer. Why would I walk away from that? I was beginning to understand what I deserved and what I didn't.

I was disappointed in myself that I'd stayed with Sean as long as I did. I deserved to be treated well, and Sean hadn't done that.

But the way that Archer looked at me. The way I could sense the change in his breathing or intensity as he stood next to me, told me this was what I deserved.

I deserved him.

15

CLEMENTINE

I stared at my computer screen, scrolling through the *must-read* book club recommendations. Some of the books I'd never heard of. Some of them looked boring and not anything I'd be interested in.

There were a few I'd jotted down in the notebook in front of me—but nothing really stood out.

So far, we had ten confirmed people coming to the first meeting next week. It had been nice, planning and arranging the book club. Maggie was wrapped up in the inn's restoration, so I'd told her that I would take over the book club details. Picking books and planning the refreshments had given me something to focus on other than the store and Dad.

Maggie had been grateful. She'd given me a big hug and told me she owed me one.

I sighed as I tapped my fingers on the countertop in front of me. I had a half an hour before the store could close. Spencer was already gone for the day. His side of the store was dark and lonely.

Leaning back in my chair, I folded my arms and glanced around. The silence was stifling me. I needed something to do, so I slipped off the stool and wandered over to the small fridge I kept behind the counter. I grabbed out a Coke. The tab made a popping sound as I opened it and brought the can to my lips.

The cool liquid stung my throat as I took a few sips and then wandered to the front of the store. I held the can in one hand and folded my free arm across my chest.

The sun had disappeared behind the trees and buildings while its remaining light painted colors across the sky. The streetlights were slowly flickering on. Families wandered down the sidewalk. Parents hand in hand with their children. I studied them as I thought of my own future.

Was something like that possible?

I wanted to believe so. But I also realized how quickly something like that could be taken away. After all, Archer had had the perfect family, and now? Nothing.

I'd been in love once, but he'd ripped my heart out. In a small town, it was hard to meet anyone. Once Jake left, I had nothing. I focused on Dad and the store, letting my hopes for the future disappear in front of me.

I was a fighter, but when it came to Jake or Dad, I stopped fighting. Their power over me held me hostage. I knew Dad didn't wanted this for me. He told me numerous times—when he remembered I was his daughter—that I needed to leave. That he could take care of things himself.

But I knew better. Sure, we lived in a small town, but he was my father. He'd taken a risk in adopting Archer and me, and I couldn't leave him like that.

I sighed as I ducked my head and shuffled back to the desk, where I started cashing out the register. I doubted anyone would come in. Ten minutes left until I could lock the doors.

Once everything was organized and closed up, I turned off the shop's light and made my way upstairs. I opened the front door and slipped my shoes off in the entryway.

"I'm home," I called out, knowing full well that Dad was most likely not going to answer. I'd checked on him a few hours ago, and he'd been fast asleep on his bed.

I stuck yesterday's leftovers into the microwave and pressed start. As I made my way down the hallway, I threw my hair up into a bun. I paused outside of Dad's room and knocked. When he didn't answer, I cracked the door and peered inside.

I expected to see a lump on the bed, but as my eyes adjusted to the darkness, no such image came into focus. Dad's bed was empty.

I threw open the door and turned on the light. My heart was pounding in my ears, and I felt dizzy as I searched his chair, his closet, and lastly, under his bed.

No Dad.

My hands shook as I scoured the rest of the apartment only to come up empty-handed.

"Dad?" I called out in a weak voice. I cleared my throat and called again. I tore through the shop, but he was nowhere to be found.

I dug my phone out of my back pocket and found Archer's number. He'd know what to do.

"Hey, Clem," he said after three rings.

"Dad's missing," I gasped. Tears stung my eyes as I blinked to lessen the pain. My heart hurt. My body hurt. My soul hurt.

"I'm outside. Be right in." Archer hung up before I could respond.

Two seconds later, I heard him jog up the stairs and barrel into the apartment.

"When was the last time you saw him?" Archer asked. His eyes were wide, and his gaze was wild as he scanned the apartment.

Tears were streaming down my face, and I couldn't find it within me to speak. Everything I tried to say came out as sobs.

Maggie appeared from behind Archer. As soon as she saw me, she crossed the room and wrapped me into a hug. "Shh. We'll find him," she said.

I was grateful for her. Archer was someone who took action, which I appreciated, but I was breaking right now. I needed someone to tell me everything was going to be okay—even if I doubted that was true.

We lived on an island. It wouldn't take much for Dad

to get lost and wander into the sea. Archer's voice filled the silence as he reported Dad's disappearance to the police. He spoke in hushed tones as he relayed information to whoever was on the other end.

"Clothes, Clem," he said, tipping his phone up and meeting my gaze.

I blinked a few times, trying to clear my head and process his words. "What?"

Archer sighed. "They need to know what he is wearing."

I nodded as I tried to recall what Dad had dressed in this morning. "Blue plaid shirt and a pair of jeans."

Archer nodded and continued his conversation.

Maggie led me over to the table, where she sat me down. Then she hurried over to the cupboard and got down a glass. After she filled it with water, she walked over and set it in front of me.

I sipped on the water as my thoughts ran wild. Archer finished up his conversation and shoved his phone into his pocket.

"I'm going to head out," he said as he spun his keys around his finger. "Call the neighbors and see if anyone else can join in."

I nodded as I moved to stand. I was going too. Archer shook his head as he held up his hand. "Stay here. Someone needs to be here if Dad wanders back."

My chest felt as if it were constricting as Archer's words settled around me. I knew what he said made sense, but I just felt so helpless. I wished I'd done something different. I wished I had heard him leave, so that I could have stopped him.

"I'll wait with her," Maggie said.

I collapsed back on the chair with my hands wrapped around the glass. They spoke in hushed tones, but I was too distracted to take notice. All I could think about was Dad wandering the streets of Magnolia with no idea who he was or where he belonged.

Archer left shortly after. The sound of the door shutting filled the silent room. I stared down at the table as I attempted to get my thoughts in order. What was I going to do? Dad was only going to get worse. Was I being selfish keeping him here?

There was a facility in Newport that Archer had looked into when Dad disappeared last year. Archer had pushed me to put him in it. They had locked doors and a twenty-four hour staff. I'd even let Archer convince me to tour it.

But when I walked through the halls, I couldn't stomach the idea of abandoning my dad there. And the fact that Archer wanted me to go through with it broke me even more. Dad had saved us from the foster system. Magnolia was his home. The thought of taking Dad and discarding him because he'd become an inconvenience was too much to bear.

I let out a sob as I buried my face into the crook of my arm. Maggie said something, and I felt her hand on my shoulder, but I couldn't hear her. My heart was too broken to speak.

When I'd cried all the tears I had, I stood and began to pace around the apartment. Maggie was quiet as she sat on the couch, watching me. I brought up my fingernail and chewed it as my mind raced.

I texted a few places to Archer. Places that I thought he might go. Archer didn't respond, which sent my anxiety through the roof. I stared down at the screen of my phone, my fingers wrapped so tight around the edges that my muscles were spasming. I willed Archer's response, but nothing came.

I felt an arm wrap around my shoulders and pull me in. Startled, I glanced up to see that Maggie was standing next to me, worry etched on her face.

"You should sit down," she said softly as she guided me to the couch.

I didn't fight her, even though every part of my body screamed for me to keep moving. As if pacing the living room floor actually did more than wear me out. It felt like if I stopped moving, that meant I'd given up on Dad.

But I was tired and too exhausted to fight Maggie. Instead, I allowed her to take control and guide me. Once I was sitting, Maggie grabbed a throw blanket and spread it across my lap.

She picked up the remote and turned the TV on. "What do you want to watch?" she asked.

I shrugged. I wasn't going to watch anything. I'd stare at the screen, but my attention would be on the door, waiting for it to open. "Whatever," I said.

Maggie scrolled through the apps and gasped when

she landed on the Korean drama app. "You watch K-dramas?" she asked, glancing over at me with her eyes wide.

I studied her. "You watch them?"

Maggie closed her lips and nodded fervently. "They are the best."

If my father hadn't been missing, I would have celebrated. But nothing felt right without Dad here. Thankfully, Maggie didn't push me further. Instead, she turned on a cooking show and declared that she was going to make me some tea.

I was too exhausted to respond. I just nodded and sunk further onto the couch. When Maggie returned, she had the plate of food I'd left in the microwave and a mug of steaming tea. She set them on the side table next to me and then settled on the floor.

She had her arm draped on the couch as she turned her attention to the screen. It was nice, having her here. It made me feel less...alone.

The chefs on the screen were all novices and were struggling with the simple cooking tasks they had been given. I found myself distracted as I watched. Even though every few minutes I would remember that Dad was missing and stare at the door, watching this show with Maggie made the wait more bearable.

It felt like an eternity, but when the sound of the door opening filled the air, my entire body tensed. I shot up from the couch and whipped my gaze over to see Archer appear in the doorway.

He met my gaze and gave me a nod. Then he turned and extended his hand out to help Dad into the house. Craig wasn't far behind them.

"Daddy," I cried out as I rushed across the room and wrapped him into a hug.

Dad was mumbling under his breath and smelled of salt, but he looked in good spirits and healthy.

"Where did you find him?" I asked as I hurried Dad inside and sat him down on a kitchen chair. I bent down and ran my gaze over him. Dad's hair was windblown, and he had a wild look in his eyes, but I couldn't see a scratch on him.

"The park," Archer said as he kicked off his shoes. He said goodbye to Craig and shut the door. He looked exhausted as he wandered into the kitchen and turned on the faucet.

"His and Mom's?" I asked. Dad proposed to Mom at Magnolia Park. It wasn't the first time he'd wandered over there.

"Janet told me to meet her there," Dad mumbled as he reached out and grabbed both of my cheeks so I would focus on him. "She's going to be mad if I'm late."

I nodded as I patted his hands. "It's okay, Dad. She will be fine with you being late," I said as I stood and made my way over to the kettle and filled it up. As I waited for the water to boil, I grabbed some gingersnap cookies from the cupboard—Dad's favorite.

When the kettle whistled, I poured the water into a mug with a tea packet and then brought it over for Dad.

Archer had found the cake that I'd made the other day and was busy eating a slice. Maggie was standing in the doorway, watching us.

With Dad settled and eating, I leaned against the counter. The room filled with silence—apart from the slurping from Dad as he drank his tea.

"Clem…" Archer finally said. His voice was filled with emotions, and I knew what he was going to say.

Tears filled my eyes as I nodded and covered my face with my hands. I didn't want to have this discussion. I knew it was going to hurt, but it was necessary.

"It's better for him." Archer took a step forward and wrapped me into a hug.

I was sobbing now. I buried my face into his chest, not caring if I was going to soak it with my snot and tears—he didn't seem to mind either.

"Dad loves you. He would never want you to worry like this for him," Archer said softly as he brought up his hand to my head and held it there.

I nodded but didn't move to step back. I needed this. I needed the reassurance that this was the right thing. For Dad. For me.

Archer held me as I cried. Once I composed myself, I took a step back and forced a smile as I looked up at him. "I'll get him ready for bed."

Archer's eyebrows were furrowed as he stared down at me. I knew he wanted to ask more, but thankfully, he held his tongue. I needed to get Dad in bed and have a good night's sleep before I was ready to talk about this more.

All he needed to know was that I was okay with moving forward with putting Dad in a facility. Which I was. No matter how much that thought broke me.

Archer studied me for a moment longer before he dropped his arms and took a step back. He glanced over at Maggie and nodded. "I'll take you back home," he said.

I gave Maggie a goodbye hug, and she told me she'd see me tomorrow. Once they left, I zeroed in on Dad, who was fading as he sat at the table. His arms were folded, and his eyes were closed. His head kept dropping. He was tired.

I was able to get him up and into his room, where I changed him into his pajamas and tucked him into bed. His snore filled the room as he fell into a deep sleep.

I quickly showered and dressed into my pajamas. As I stood in my room, my gaze kept drifting over to Dad's room. There was no way I was going to be able to sleep on my bed. The worry that Dad would wake up again and disappear for good had taken over me.

So I grabbed my comforter and pillow and padded quietly into Dad's room, where I spread them out onto the floor. If he tried to leave, he'd trip over me, waking me up.

Even though the floor was cold and hard, I didn't care. I was going to protect Dad, no matter the cost. His safety was more important to me than my comfort.

Eventually, I got tired of fighting sleep—or worrying—and my body finally relaxed enough to fall into a restless sleep.

Tomorrow, my life was going to change, and I needed

all the cards stacked in my favor. Showing up at the facility sleep-deprived and exhausted did not sound like a winning combination.

Dad was going to need an alert Clementine tomorrow, and I'd be that person for him.

It was the least I could do.

16

MAGGIE

Archer was quiet as he drove me back to the inn. I kept glancing over at him, wanting to say something, but nothing came to mind. Instead, every comment I could think of sounded trite and disingenuous. So I kept my lips pressed closed as I studied the dark world around us.

The inn came into view, and exhaustion took over. Archer pulled into the parking lot and let his truck idle. His focus was forward, and his hands rested on the steering wheel. His shoulders were tight and I could tell that he had the weight of the world on them.

"It'll be okay," I whispered. I wanted to say something —anything—to help.

Archer didn't move to acknowledge my words. He just sat there as rigid as a board. Not sure what I was supposed to do, I reached down and grabbed the door handle.

"Wait," Archer said. His voice was low and caught me

off guard. I obeyed and watched as he opened his door, jumped down, and came around to open my door.

He extended his hand, and I took it. He helped me down, and as soon as my feet hit the ground, I expected him to let go, but he didn't. Instead, his fingers lingered with mine. Seconds felt like hours as he held my hand. His gaze was downturned as if he were studying them.

Then, in slow motion, he uncurled his fingers and my hand dropped to my side. He cleared his throat and then glanced up at me. I offered him a soft smile, hoping to tell him that I was okay with what had happened even though, deep down, I was confused.

He stood there for a few seconds before he reached out and pressed his hand on my lower back, guiding me toward the front door. I obeyed, and we walked side by side up the porch stairs to the front door.

I fiddled in my purse for my keys as Archer stood next to me. Once I located them, I slipped one into the lock but then paused. I didn't want to go inside. I didn't want him to leave. I wanted a lot more than what we had.

I wanted him.

I turned to face him. "I'm happy your dad's safe," I said.

He met my gaze and held it for a moment. Then he pushed his hand through his hair as he turned to glance at the ocean. The moon was high in the sky and reflected off the water.

"Me too," he said, softly.

I folded my arms across my chest and took in a deep breath. "Do you think Clementine's going to be okay? She seemed pretty shaken up." My thoughts returned to my friend, and my chest squeezed with worry for her. I wish I knew how to help—how to make this better for her. But I didn't know how.

"It's good that you're here. She needs the support." He blew out his breath as he turned his focus back to me. "I've been lacking in that department." He shoved his hands into his front pockets.

I shook my head. "You've been really supportive. It's good that she has you around," I said as I reached out and allowed my fingers to brush his arm. Warmth exploded from my fingertips and raced up my arm. My heart pounded hard, and my breathing deepened as I glanced up to meet his gaze.

The intensity of his stare caused my knees to weaken. His shoulders had rounded, and I watched as he leaned in. I'd never realized until this moment how perfect his lips were. They were full and kissable.

"Thanks for spending the day with me," he said. His voice had deepened, and I reveled in the sound as it sent shivers across my skin.

"Of course. Thanks for taking me around."

He studied me. My cheeks flushed, but I didn't back down. Breaking this connection between us was the last thing I wanted to do. A silence fell around us, and I wondered if he felt the anticipation as much as I did.

I took courage in the fact that he didn't move. He didn't pull away. He just stood there, his warmth washing over me. I wanted to close my eyes. I wanted to lean in. To kiss him with the passion that was coursing through me with every beat of my heart.

The breeze picked up, and suddenly, my hair was swirling around. I blinked a few times, and just as I reached up to brush away the strands that had landed on my face, my fingers touched Archer's. He'd had the same idea.

I felt frozen in place as I watched his gaze intensify when his fingers brushed my cheeks and then my ears as he tucked my hair behind them. I expected him to drop his hand, but he never did. Instead, his fingers lingered on my ear as he turned his attention back to me.

Out of instinct, I felt myself lean into him. I wanted him to know what I wanted. I beckoned him to kiss me.

His gaze dropped to my lips as he slipped his hand to cradle my cheek, his fingers threading through my hair. Then slowly, gently, he leaned in and brushed his lips against mine.

My entire body responded as I leaned into him. His kiss only lasted seconds before he pulled away. I opened my eyes to see what was the matter. Archer stood there, his gaze searching mine.

Not wanting him to regret what he'd done, not wanting him to think I didn't want this, I fisted his shirt and pulled him back to me, crushing my lips against his. I wanted—needed—his kiss.

As if taking that as his cue, he wrapped his arm around my waist and pulled me against him with such need, such desire, that I gasped. I was brought back to the night he hugged me. Except this time, we were both drowning and hanging onto the other for survival.

I slipped my hands behind his neck and threaded my fingers through his hair as I rose up onto my tiptoes to deepen the kiss. Archer wrapped his other arm around me, and suddenly, I was airborne. He brought me over to the railing and set me on it.

I parted my lips, and our kiss deepened. There was a need that we were both looking to fulfill, and we'd managed to find it in each other. Our arms, our hands, our lips found the answers to our question.

I could have kissed Archer all night. The last thing I wanted was for him to leave. I'd never felt so complete as I did right then. Magnolia. The inn. Archer. Clementine. I felt like this was the home I'd been searching for. I was where I was meant to be.

Here. Wrapped in Archer's arms.

I groaned as he pulled away. The cadence of our breath matched as he tipped his forehead to rest it on mine. I kept my eyes closed as we stood there. No one spoke. It was as if we were lingering in the moment we'd shared.

I slid my hands down his chest and fiddled with the hem of his shirt. He pulled back, and I opened my eyes to see him studying me. I gave him a soft smile, and he responded by reaching up and tucking my hair behind my ear. When he finished, his fingers lingered on my skin, and I reached up to hold his hand.

"I should go," he said. His voice was gruff, and I giggled at the sound. It was amazing.

"Okay," I whispered.

Archer met my gaze, studying me for a moment before passion flashed in his gaze, and he pulled me into him once more. His kiss was deeper this time. I could feel his want. His desire. He pulled me off the railing and pushed me back until I was pressed against the siding of the house.

He kept one hand securely on my lower back and his other hand went up to rest on the wall behind me. As if he needed the support of the wall. Though, with the way my body was responding to his kiss, I needed its support.

Suddenly, he growled and pulled away. He took a few steps back as he ran his hand through his hair. It took him a moment before he raised his gaze to meet mine. "I'm going to go," he said. The heat of his gaze sent my heart racing.

I chewed my bottom lip as I nodded. "Okay."

He studied me for a moment longer before he turned and bounded down the porch stairs and over to his truck. He climbed in, and as soon as he started the engine, he pulled out of the parking spot. Just before he turned to head down the main road, he stopped as he raised his gaze up to meet mine.

He held it for a second. I could see his want to stay flash through his gaze. I gave him a wave, and he did the same. Then he blinked a few times and pulled out onto the street. I waited on the porch as I reveled in the memory of Archer's arms around me. Of his lips against mine.

I stared out at the ocean. I couldn't stop the smile or

the completeness I felt at this moment. I wrapped my arms around my chest and made my way into the inn. I couldn't wait to go to sleep. I was desperate for morning to come. I wanted to see Archer more than anything.

I gasped as I walked into the kitchen. I'd completely forgotten that they had gutted it today. Everything was down to drywall and underlayment. I wanted to get a drink, but there was no sink to use. The cupboards were all pulled down, and I wondered where they had put my meager amount of dishes.

Shaking my head, I made my way into my bedroom. I'd worry about all of that tomorrow. I drank from the bathroom faucet and changed into my pajamas. I was ready for sleep.

As soon as my head hit the pillow, my eyes drifted closed. My entire body felt warm as I recalled our kiss. I'd never felt this happy or this at peace. If all of the horrible experiences I'd gone through led up to this—my move to Magnolia—then I would happily go through it all again.

My body began to relax as sleep took over. My thoughts drifted to fate, and I couldn't help the smile that tugged at my lips. Apparently, she wasn't angry with me anymore. Things were finally looking up.

My life was changing, and I was ready for it.

And the fact that Penny had every intention of selling the inn? Well, I was just going to forget that for the time being.

———

The sun burst through my window the next morning. In my haste to get to bed the night before, I'd forgotten to close my drapes. But I didn't mind. The light matched my mood.

I stretched my arms over my head as I shimmied farther down under my comforter. My body was relaxed and content. I was going to lie here for a few more minutes, and then I'd get up.

It was hard, but I finally forced myself out of bed at 7:30. I was sure I could have stayed there forever, but things needed to get done.

I padded into the bathroom and started the shower. After I was clean, I wrapped a towel around my body and then twisted another up with my hair. I slipped into my room and over to the door.

I needed some coffee before I finished getting ready.

When I got to the kitchen, I was instantly reminded that finding my coffee pot might be more difficult than I'd originally anticipated. Five minutes later, I'd located all of my kitchenware. The guys had stacked it neatly in the corner of the large dining room.

I reached down to grab the coffee machine just as the front door opened. I yelped and cradled the pot against my chest as I whipped my gaze over to see Archer standing there with a small box of pastries and two cups of coffee.

His eyes were wide as he ran his gaze over me. My skin felt as if it were on fire as I stood there, frozen to the spot.

There were voices sounding from behind him, and that seemed to snap him out of his shock. He turned and grabbed the door as he started pushing whoever it was back out onto the porch.

"What the—Archer!" said a voice that sounded like Tom's.

"Wait out here," Archer said as he shut the door and then turned to face me. His eyebrows were knit together. "What are you trying to do to me?" he asked, his voice low as he studied me.

My entire body flushed as I set the coffee pot onto the table next to me. I wrapped my arms around my chest. The fear of my towel falling down in front of Archer crashed into me.

I offered him an apologetic smile as I began to pad over to the hallway.

"Wait."

His voice caused me to stop. I stared at the floor, wondering what he was thinking. Besides the parts that my towel covered, I was exposed. He could see my legs. My back. My shoulders.

Was he disgusted?

At least when I was clothed, he could imagine that I looked better than I did.

Gathering my courage, I turned to look at him. His gaze was dark and hard to read as he stared at me.

I could feel his gaze as it roamed over me. I chewed on my lip, trying to stop the excuses that I would give to Sean every time his snide comments would leave his lips about my appearance.

I didn't want Archer to know how insecure I was about my body. If he wasn't thinking these things, I didn't want to put them there.

Slowly, he made his way across the room. I sucked in my breath as he neared, fearing what he was going to do once he got close. Kissing me in the darkness last night was one thing. Seeing my body in the light of day was a whole other thing.

He stopped, inches from my body. I kept my gaze down, hoping he would just get this interaction over with. Suddenly, I felt the pad of his finger slip under my chin as he directed my face upward. As much as I tried not to, my gaze shifted to meet his.

I sucked in my breath when I saw what resided in his gaze.

Heat.

Longing.

Desire.

Things that Sean never showed me.

"Is this the body you were so scared of yesterday. The one you said your ex…" He paused like he was trying to recall my words. "Was disappointed in?"

Tears filled my eyes. I hated that I hated myself like I did. I wanted to have confidence, but I didn't.

My gaze must have answered him because suddenly, his lips were on my shoulder and he was pressing soft kisses into my skin. I gasped, the feeling of warmth shocking me.

"He's an idiot. From what I'm seeing." Then he pulled back to meet my gaze. "And not seeing." His dragged his fingers along the towel tied around my chest. "I'm going to like every part of you." His fingers slipped from my towel to continue across my skin.

"And the things that you fear I won't like." He brought his lips down to kiss my upper arm before he straightened out my arm to kiss the sensitive part of my elbow, then wrist, and then the top of my hand. He gripped my fingers and pulled me into him where he wrapped his arms around me and held me close to his chest. "I'm definitely going to like, because they are you," he whispered as he brought his lips down to my ear.

Then he released his hold on me and dropped to the ground in front of me. Heat raced to my cheeks as I watched him. He gently touched my ankle, then calf. Slowly, he brought his lips to my knee and then his hands wrapped around my thigh.

I wanted to push him away. I wanted to run and hide in my room. These were the parts of my body that I never wanted people to see. I was ashamed of them.

And to have a man I was quickly falling in love with, up close and personal with my flaws, scared me.

But tightness in his grip told me, he wanted me to go no where. He started tracing his finger along my thigh, sending shivers across my skin. I studied what he was doing and realized, he was tracing the lines of stretch marks I had there.

Before I could stop him, he leaned in and pressed his lips to them. My heart pounded in my chest. Was this real?

"Archer…" I whispered, unsure of what else to say.

He pulled back and met my gaze. I was sure he could see my fear like I could see his desire. Nothing had changed. If anything, the way his jaw muscles were flexing and the way his fingers lingered on my leg, he wanted me.

Like I wanted him.

Two knocks on the door started us. We both turned toward the door that Archer had come through.

"Can we come in now?" Tom asked.

Archer straightened as a sheepish look passed over his face. "Just a minute," he yelled toward the door as he wrapped an arm around my waist and pulled me close. "Go get dressed. Your body is mine and I'm not sharing it with Tom or anyone else."

My entire body felt like an inferno, but I nodded and gripped my towel closer to my body as I hurried toward the hallway. I could feel the warmth of his gaze as I disappeared into my room.

My heart was racing as I shut the door and leaned against it, tipping my face upward. An uncontrollable giggle exploded through me, and I had to cover my mouth to muffle it.

I hurried to dress in a tank top and shorts. I braided my damp hair and applied a little makeup. When I was presentable, I pulled open my door and made my way through the house until I found where the voices were coming from.

Archer was talking to Tom. They were standing over some plans, and Archer was pointing to the diagram of the cupboards. I stood back and watched them.

Archer must have felt my gaze because, a moment later, he glanced up. When his gaze met mine, he smiled. It was smooth and melted my insides just a bit. He studied me for a moment before Tom said something, drawing Archer's attention back over.

They continued speaking, and I began to feel like a creeper just standing there. So I turned and slipped from the room. After our impromptu day playing hooky, I was behind on the things I needed to get done.

The floor sander had been delivered and was standing in the middle of the living room, waiting for me. I walked over to it and bent down to unwind the cord. Before I finished, I felt a hand on my arm. I glanced behind me just in time to see Archer pull me up.

My heart began to pound as I turned to face him. He cradled my cheek as he pressed his lips against mine. The kiss was less desperate than it had been yesterday, but it still sent jolts of electricity through my body.

After a few seconds, he pulled away but kept close to me, his hand resting on my lower back. "Good morning," he said as he smiled down at me.

My cheeks flushed as I smiled up at him. "Good morning."

He held my gaze as his thumb stroked my cheek. He furrowed his brow as he studied me. "Did you sleep well?"

I bit my lip and nodded. It felt so good, being held by him.

Voices neared, and Archer pulled back so he was no longer touching me. But he remained close as he shoved his hands into his front pockets. I smoothed down my hair and attempted to cool the temperature of my body.

"How was Clementine when she woke up?"

Archer nodded. "She's okay. Called the facility today. They had an opening, so we're going with Dad there tonight." He paused. "You should call her. She could really use a friend right now."

My heart broke for Clementine. I nodded. "I will."

Archer smiled, and my heart soared. We stood there, studying each other for a moment longer before he nodded at the sander. "Want me to show you how to use this?"

I blew out my breath as I shifted my focus. "Definitely."

He took his time explaining how to sand with the grain and how to get a smooth finish. I was content just standing there, listening to the smooth inflections of his voice. I grabbed the handles of the sander according to his directions, and my entire body responded when he wrapped his arms around me to accurately show me.

He was warm, and I fit next to him like I belonged there. Eventually, Tom called him away, and I was left to sand the floor by myself. I got lost in my thoughts as the vibrations from the machine thrummed through my body.

I spent the whole day working on the flooring. My hands were sore. My legs were sore. I was covered in dust. But I'd never been happier.

This was where I belonged.

CLEMENTINE

I was having a hard time keeping my emotions together. I spent the entire day either crying in the bathroom or being on the verge of tears. I had a bunch of wadded up tissues in my pocket, and I was having a hard time telling which were used and which were clean.

The day went by too fast, and suddenly, Michelle was standing in front of me. Her expression was soft as she ran her gaze over me. I could only assume Archer called her and let her know my status. I hated that she was pitying me. It only confirmed what I thought—that I looked pathetic.

"Hey," I said through my sniffles. Her sympathetic gaze was only making things worse. I was struggling to keep my feelings inside, and one look at her caused them to bubble up.

She knew what I was sad about, which only reminded me why I was upset.

"I stocked the shelves. I was just about to get things together for the evening cash out, but..." My tears welled up, and my voice just stopped working. I stared at the paperwork in front of me. I knew I had written on it. I could see the black swirls through my tears, but I couldn't make out any of the writing.

By the time I'd gathered my thoughts enough to speak, I forgot what I was talking about. I felt Michelle's arm wrap around me as she pulled me into a side hug.

"I can take it from here. Go spend some time with your dad," she said softly.

I didn't have the will to fight. So I nodded, wiped my tears with the back of my hand, and pulled away. "Thanks," I mumbled.

"Of course."

I didn't look back as I made my way to the storage room, through the back entry, and up the stairs. Spencer had offered to sit with Dad while I worked. When I asked about the work he had to do, he said he'd stay late tonight. I could tell he was struggling with our decision. He wasn't an emotional man, but from the way his neck muscles tightened and the redness in his eyes, I could tell he was trying to muscle down his sadness as much as I was.

When I opened the apartment door, I heard the low voice of Spencer. I quietly shut the door behind me and slipped off my shoes. I peered into the living room to find

Dad sitting in his chair with his eyes closed while Spencer read to him.

I quickly covered my mouth with my hand to stifle the sob that almost escaped. I didn't want to interrupt their moment with my tears. Thankfully, neither noticed me, and I was able to escape to my room, where I shut the door and flung myself onto the bed.

I let the tears flow. I needed to cry out every ounce of liquid I had inside of me if I was going to survive this evening with any amount of dignity. Dad would sense that something was wrong with me, and I didn't want him to feel stressed about his new place.

A soft knock sounded on my door ten minutes later. I'd finally composed myself and was now sitting on my bed with my back against the headboard. I was picking at the corner of the tissue I had in my hand.

I glanced up. "Come in," I said. My throat was raw from the tears and snot, so my voice was hoarse.

The door opened, and I watched as Maggie peeked around it. Her gaze fell on me, and her forehead furrowed as she pushed in and shut the door behind her. Seeing her expression made me want to start crying again. Thankfully, I didn't have anything left, and I was able to accept her hug without covering her in tears.

"Hey," she said as she pulled back and reached down to hold my hand. "How are you holding up?"

My throat felt as if it were constricting, but I managed to hold it together. "I'm okay." I blew out my breath. "Just worried about Dad. I don't want him to think we're getting rid of him or anything."

Maggie's expression softened as she nodded. "He won't think that. I'm sure he understands."

My stomach sunk as I thought of abandoning Dad at the home. I wanted to believe that he would understand. That if he were mentally here, he would be telling us to take him—like he'd done numerous times before we lost him to the disease. He always made us promise that as soon as he became a burden to us, we'd take him to an assisted living place.

In the moment, I'd brush off his words by telling him he wasn't going to get worse, to which he would laugh. But in the serious moments of our conversations, he would take me by the shoulders and stare deep into my eyes. Then he would make me swear to obey his wish.

I hated that he knew I'd be weak and eventually need to bring him to a facility. I was sure he didn't want me to carry the guilt, but it was painful to think he knew I wouldn't be able to take care of him.

Pulling away from Maggie, I sighed and stood, walking over to the trash can and throwing away my tissue. Then I tipped my face toward the ceiling and gathered my strength.

"Archer here?" I asked.

"Yes," Maggie said as she stood and began walking around my room, studying the pictures on my walls and items on my shelves. Her lips were tipped up into a smile as she paused on the family picture we had taken when Archer and I were in high school.

I nodded as I studied my reflection in the mirror. I patted the skin under my eyes and grabbed another tissue to wipe at my nose. After throwing my hair up into a ponytail, I smoothed out my shirt and cleared my throat.

"I think I'm ready," I said. Maggie glanced over at me and nodded.

I'd spent the morning gathering Dad's belongings and packing them into suitcases. Yolanda, the admissions specialist, called me right at eight this morning. I'd called and left her a message last night at Archer's bidding. He knew I would change my mind, but if the home knew I was bringing Dad, I would have to follow through.

He was right.

Yolanda said she'd send their movers over this afternoon to pick up his big items, but I would need to pack his smaller belongings and bring them with us. It was hard, boxing up Dad's stuff. We'd done it ten years ago when Mom passed away. There were items I kept, but for the most part, I had to get rid of everything she'd owned.

It was like losing her all over again.

I had a feeling it was going to be just as hard with Dad.

Maggie wrapped her arm around my shoulder as we walked through the door and out to the hall. Archer was leaning against the wall with his legs extended, hands were in his front pockets, head tipped back, and eyes closed.

He was listening to Spencer read. I had to admit, it was the calm we needed before the intensity of dropping Dad off.

Archer must have heard us because he straightened and glanced over. He gave me a sympathetic look as he crossed the space between us and wrapped his arms around me, pulling me into one of his crushing hugs.

I nodded as I buried my face into his shoulder. His hugs reminded me of Dad, and right now, this was what I needed.

"It'll be okay, Clem," he said as he reached up and cradled my head.

I took in a deep breath. Archer smelled like salt mixed with the outdoors—just like Dad. I pulled back and gave him a small smile. It was all I could muster. If I was going to survive this evening, I needed to get a handle on my emotions.

For Dad.

"Ready?" I asked.

Archer nodded. "I loaded Dad's boxes into the back of the truck."

I blew out my breath. "Good." I glanced over at Maggie. "Will you come with us?"

Maggie reached down and grabbed my hand. "Of course. If you want me there, I'll come."

We made our way into the living room, and Spencer raised his gaze to meet ours. I gave him a solemn nod, and despite his prickly personality, I saw his eyes redden as he glanced over at Dad, who had fallen asleep on his chair.

His head was tipped to the side, and I could see his deep breaths.

Spencer closed the book he was reading and set it on the side table next to him. Then he stood, patted Dad on the shoulder, whispered something that sounded like "See you soon, friend," and hurried from the apartment.

With him gone, I nodded to Archer, and we both rounded the chair and knelt down in front of Dad. I rested my hand on his. "Dad," I whispered.

When that didn't wake him, Archer sat on the couch and shook Dad's shoulder. "Dad," he said.

Dad snorted as he startled awake. His eyes widened as he took in me and Archer. Then a slow, familiar smile spread across his lips. "Hey, guys," he said. He reached his hand out and cradled my cheek. "Hey, sissy."

My eyes filled with tears at the nickname he'd given me. I felt my resolve waning as he sat there, smiling. I could do this. I could watch over him. I'd just need to be more diligent. I just needed to work harder.

"Clem," Archer's voice cut through my thoughts. I turned to see his concerned expression as he studied me. "It's for the best," he whispered.

A tear slid down my cheek as I moved my focus back to Dad. I knew what Archer was saying. A glimpse of hope didn't mean what I so desperately wanted it to mean. Dad had become too much for me to handle. He needed to be in a place that would care for him and keep him safe.

That place wasn't with me.

Despite my desire to pull back and call foul on all of

this, I held Dad's hand as I stood. Dad didn't seem to question what was going on. Instead, he rose from his seat.

Another tear slipped down my cheek, and I raised my hand to angrily wipe it away. I didn't want to cry in front of Dad. I didn't want him to worry about me.

I held Dad's hand as we walked over to the front door and helped him with his shoes and jacket. He didn't look alarmed as I slipped his hat on his head. Instead, his gaze was full of love as he stared down at me.

"Why are you crying, sissy?" he asked.

I stifled a sob as I forced a smile. "I'm just..." What was I supposed to say? I wasn't happy. I was breaking inside. But I didn't want to put that on him. So I wrapped him into a hug and said the only truth that came to my mind. "I love you."

Dad's big arms surrounded me as he crushed me to his chest. "I love you, too."

Suddenly I felt the pressure of another set of arms. I looked up to see Archer had engulfed us both. As I met Archer's gaze, I gave him a smile and watched as a tear slid down his cheek.

My big, stronger-than-life brother was breaking as well.

We stood there, hugging, for what felt like hours. If I were honest with myself, I didn't want to pull away. Reality was on the other side of this hug, and for right now, I wanted to ignore it.

Eventually, we'd leave. We'd climb into the car and drive across the bridge to the assisted living home. I'd unpack Dad in his new room, and eventually, I'd walk out, leaving him behind.

I buried my face in the soft flannel of Dad's shirt. I took in a deep breath, memorizing the smell and feel. I would have stayed there forever, but Archer finally stepped back and declared that we needed to leave. Their intake was only open until seven, and if we wanted to get there before they closed up, we needed to hurry.

I sniffled as I nodded and pulled away. I linked arms with Dad as I helped him down the stairs and into Archer's truck. Dad and I sat in the back, and Archer and Maggie sat in the front seats.

Archer picked Neil Diamond—Dad's favorite artist— to listen to. I could see the smile on Dad's lips as he tapped his fingers to the beat of the music. When we got to the home, I helped Dad down and held onto him as we walked inside.

The facility was nice enough. Betty was the nurse who greeted us with a warm smile and a soft voice. She was older, mid-fifties if I had to guess. She was wearing bright-pink scrubs, and her greying hair was pulled up into a bun and secured with a claw clip.

She was patient when I asked her questions, reassuring me several times that the doors required a code to open and that Dad would be well looked after. When I surveyed the other residents there, none of them looked miserable. A couple of women sat in the corner, playing a card game. I wasn't sure if they all knew what they were playing, but they were enjoying themselves, which I took as a positive sign.

By the time we'd unpacked Dad's belongings into the drawers and provided shelves, it was time to go. Dad was already in his pajamas and had settled into his bed. Archer didn't seem as determined to stay as I did. He was hovering near the door, stifling his yawn.

I appreciated that he wasn't pushing me, and I knew that I couldn't stay here forever. So I leaned in and gave Dad one more kiss on the forehead and squeeze of his hand before turning and nodding at Archer. He smiled as he nodded back. He crossed the room, gave Dad a kiss and a hug, and then hurried from the room.

As I made my way into the hallway, I felt Maggie's arm surround my shoulders. She'd been so quiet and patient while we were here. She'd helped unpack Dad's things and then had stayed close to the wall.

I wrapped my arm around her waist and leaned into her. "Thanks for coming," I said.

Maggie squeezed my shoulder with her hand. "Of course. That's what friends are for."

I sighed. Exhaustion took over my body, and the only thing I wanted to do was crawl into my bed and fall asleep.

The drive back was quiet. I sat up front, staring out the window at the world as it passed by. By the time Archer pulled into the back parking lot, I was almost asleep. I mumbled a quick goodbye to Maggie and Archer and made my way upstairs.

Archer pulled out of his parking spot as the exterior door shut behind me. He'd driven Maggie here and wanted to get her home. Then he'd be back.

I didn't think much of it as I sleepily climbed the stairs and kicked off my shoes. I didn't even undress. I crawled into bed and pulled the covers up to my chin as my eyes became heavy, and I drifted off.

MAGGIE

Archer was quiet the entire drive back to the inn. I peeked over at him a few times just to see that his jaw was set and his gaze was distant. I thought about speaking to him, breaking the silence, but then decided against it.

Clementine seemed like a person who needed to talk things through, but Archer was the complete opposite. I had a feeling that, even though it didn't seem like it, he had a lot going on in his mind and in his heart.

Plus, I was comfortable with just sitting next to him, enjoying his company. If he needed me for support, I was more than happy to provide that as well.

Suddenly, the feeling of a hand surrounding mine drew my attention over. I glanced down to see Archer had wrapped my hand up in his. My heart took off racing, and I couldn't stop the smile that pulled at my lips. I twisted my hand until my palm was facing up and entwined my fingers with his.

We drove the rest of the way in silence. The warmth of our hands said what our mouths didn't. I'd never felt so at peace with someone as I did with Archer. We were both broken, hurting people, and yet, we'd found the strength we were missing in each other.

The paths we'd taken to find each other were painful, but that pain dulled in comparison to how I felt about him. We were each the healing that the other person needed.

When he pulled into the inn's parking lot, he put the car in park and idled the engine. Then he turned to face me. The look in his eyes took my breath away as I held his gaze.

"Thanks for coming tonight," he said as he ran his thumb across my knuckles. That movement sent shivers up my arm, and feelings exploded in my chest.

All I could do was nod. My emotions were heightened, and I feared I might say something stupid. Archer studied me for a moment. Then he reached out with his free hand to cradle my cheek. He pulled closer, and I responded by doing the same.

The kiss that we shared was gentle and sweet. There wasn't the need that had been there when he'd kissed me on the porch. He needed comfort, and I was more than willing to show him that I'd be that person for him.

When he broke our kiss, we remained close. Our foreheads were pressed together, and from my hazy gaze, I could see that his eyes were closed. Our breaths matched as we remained there, feeling.

I could have stayed there the rest of the night, but I didn't want Clementine to be alone tonight. Not with everything she just went through. So I reached up and wrapped my hand around Archer's and slowly pulled it from my cheek. I squeezed his fingers as I pulled away.

"I should get to bed," I whispered.

Archer glanced up at me. His brow was furrowed as he stared at me. I could see his desire to stay. It sent butterflies racing in my stomach. As much as I wanted to oblige, I was worried about Clementine.

"Go. I'll be fine. Clementine needs her family around her." I pulled on the door handle. The outside breeze carried into the cab of the truck and surrounded me. It was fresh and salty—a smell that I was beginning to love.

Archer didn't say anything. Instead, he nodded and turned to grip the steering wheel. I smiled as I jumped down and held the door open. "I'll see you tomorrow?" I asked, leaning into the cab. He turned to study me.

"Yep," he said, and then a few seconds later, he gave me a wink and a soft smile. "I'll be here bright and early."

I laughed as I stepped away from the truck and slammed the door. I watched as he pulled out of the parking lot, made his way down the street, and disappeared around the corner.

Now alone, I blew out my breath as I shouldered my

purse and walked across the parking lot. Once I was inside, I wandered back to my room, where I washed my face and changed into my pajamas.

I curled up in bed with a book, but I didn't last long. Just before my eyes closed for the final time, I slipped my book onto my nightstand and shut off my light.

———

The rest of the week went by quickly. Between working on the inn and planning our first book club meeting, I had very little time to breathe, much less think.

Without her Dad around, Clementine needed to keep busy. She was cleaning the top shelf of one of the racks when I walked into the hardware store Friday afternoon. I'd left Archer at the inn with the guys. They were putting the finishing touches on the brand-new kitchen. It was modern and beautiful, and I couldn't imagine it looking any better.

With the bones in place, it was time for me to work my magic. I was hoping to go into Newport with Clementine to pick our kitchenware and decorations so the room didn't look so empty.

"Hey," I said as I walked over to the ladder and peered up at Clementine.

She glanced down at me, blowing her hair from her forehead. A smile spread across her lips as she set down her rag and climbed down. "Hey." She dabbed at her forehead with the outside of her wrist as she glanced around.

"Are you ready?"

Clementine nodded as she pushed her hair back. "Yep. Let me change into something that's not covered in dust and sweat."

I nodded as she walked away.

"I'll be back in under five minutes," she called over her shoulder as she disappeared into the back room.

I kept busy by studying some of the items in front of me. Michelle came over, and we made small talk until Clementine showed up with a big smile. She'd changed into a black t-shirt and shorts. Her hair was brushed and hanging down to the middle of her back.

"Ready?" she asked.

I nodded, said goodbye to Michelle, and followed her out of the store. We drove thirty minutes into Newport to Home Goods. It seemed to be exactly the kind of store I needed.

After stepping inside and staring around at everything, I determined that it *was* exactly the kind of store I needed.

We shopped for hours, and when we were done, my feet felt as if they were going to fall off. Thankfully, they offered delivery, so after I paid, Clementine and I walked out of the store empty-handed.

Which was nice. There was no way I had the energy to pack everything up and unload it once we got back to the island. We settled into the car, the cool air blasting from the vents.

I pulled out of the parking spot as Clementine announced, "I'm starving."

I nodded. "Same. Should we get some dinner?"

Clementine shot me a smile. "I know just the place."

Clementine directed me to a small restaurant on the beach. It was quaint and quiet, and when we walked in, the food smelled divine and made my stomach rumble.

"You're a genius," I said.

Clementine laughed as we followed after the hostess, who sat us on the deck overlooking the ocean. The darkness of the world around us mixed with the sounds of the waves and brought peace to my soul.

We settled in. I ordered a Diet Coke, and Clementine got a wine cooler. We laughed and talked about the day and the book club, which was holding its first meeting tomorrow.

"I'm nervous," Clementine admitted after the waitress took our drink orders.

I furrowed my brow. "Why? It'll be fun."

She shrugged. "I guess I just feel the pressure to make it great. After all, it feels almost like a tribute to my mom. And with Dad gone…" Her voice drifted off. She picked up her napkin and dabbed the corner of her eye.

I shot her a sympathetic glance, which she waved off.

"It's okay. He's doing so well there. Betty calls me every day she works to update me. Apparently, he's considered quite the catch among the ladies there." She laughed and shrugged. "Which was no surprise."

I nodded. "I can see that."

Our conversation grew quiet. I could see that Clementine was wrestling with something. I wanted to help; I just wasn't sure how.

"I'm nervous too," I said after I took a sip of my Coke. "My mom's expected soon, and I'm worried that she won't think we've progressed like we need to."

Clementine studied me. "The inn looks amazing. You and Archer have really worked hard on it. I can't imagine she won't like it."

I shrugged. "But my mother is obsessed with perfection. I'm worried we won't have the same tastes."

"So what? It's amazing, and she'd be ridiculous not to be happy with it."

I blew out my breath just as the waitress approached with our drinks. When she left, Clementine furrowed her brow as she met my gaze.

"So, when your mom gets here and signs off on the improvements—which she definitely will—what does that mean for the inn?"

My stomach flipped as I glanced out toward the ocean. I'd been thinking a lot about that lately. The original plan had been to fix up the inn to sell. Then I could take the proceeds to start Studio Red. But the longer I stayed here, the greater my desire was to make Magnolia my permanent home.

I just wasn't sure what Penny would think of that.

"Well, she'll want to sell. That has always been her intention," I said slowly. I didn't want to alarm Clementine or Archer—I was still planning on convincing Penny to let me run Magnolia Inn. But in case she dug in her heels, I didn't want to blindside them.

Clementine snorted. "Doesn't she realize how much more she'd make from running it? Magnolia Inn is an institution around here. Once it's up and running, you won't have a hard time filling the rooms."

I nodded as I chewed on my straw. All of her points made sense. I could see it, but my mother was another beast. If I ran the inn, that would make her an investor. Plus, with her hesitation to even tell me about the inn— about Dorthy—I doubted keeping the place in the family was what she wanted to do.

Until I knew why she'd had a falling out with my grandmother, I couldn't guess what she was going to do. Her reasoning could be petty or justified.

I had a sinking feeling that she might not ever tell me no matter how much I wanted to know.

The waitress brought us our food. I got lobster ravioli, and Clementine got fish and chips. We ate and talked— keeping our conversation light. Clementine ran over the menu for the book club tomorrow. She was making mini lobster quiches for the main dish. She had a fruit and vegetable platter planned, and she'd bought mini dough- nuts and eclairs.

We were going to have fresh-squeezed lemonade and wine for drinks. Even though I was currently stuffing my face full of food, all of the items she mentioned had my mouth watering.

Even if it was just a meeting to pick our first book, the

food sounded amazing. We were going to retain people with the menu alone.

We finished our dinner, and the plates were picked up. I was stuffed beyond belief, so when Clementine leaned in and said she had one more store to hit up, I agreed. Anything to get my body up and moving.

We took a short drive over to a small boutique called Missy Mae. I parked along the road, and we both climbed out. Clementine held open the door as I walked inside. It was an adorable store. Racks of clothing lined the walls, and in the back were floor-to-ceiling shelves that held boxes of shoes.

Clementine walked up to the register and started talking to a woman who I later learned was named Winny and was the owner of the store. She told Clementine she had her order ready and to wait there.

I leaned against the counter as I turned to face Clementine. "What did you order?" I asked.

Clementine glanced over at me with a wicked smile. "A surprise for tomorrow."

I furrowed my brow. "From a boutique?"

Clementine nodded. Just as she did, Winny appeared. Well, a walking stack of shoeboxes appeared. Winny peeked out from behind them and gave us a smile. "Want me to bring these out to your car?" she asked.

Clementine and I hurried to help her. I took a few boxes, and Clementine took a few more—enough to uncover Winny. I glanced over at Clementine as we walked out to my car.

Once we stacked then in the back seat, I slipped the lid off one of the boxes and busted up laughing. Nestled in the protective paper was a pair of red stiletto heels. I glanced up to see Clementine's wide smile.

"Nice touch," I said as I slipped the lid back on.

Clementine shrugged as she thanked Winny, and we both climbed into the car. "I hope you don't mind, but I stole your size from your shoe the other day."

I glanced over at her as I started the engine. "You got everyone's size?"

Clementine buckled. "Yep. Well, everyone who promised to come." Then she paused. "You owe me thirty."

I nodded as I pressed on my blinker and merged into traffic. "I'll settle up with you when we get home."

We spent the rest of the drive talking about tomorrow and what we were going to do next week. There was still so much about Magnolia that I hadn't explored. Planning an outing with Clementine only made my heart hurt that much more.

What if Penny decided not to let me run Magnolia Inn? What if staying in Magnolia just wasn't in the cards for me? After all, I was jobless without the inn or Penny's investment in my design company. Would I be able to find a place here to employ me?

I knew Clementine would make an effort to take me in, but I couldn't impose on her like that. It wasn't like the hardware store was extremely busy, and I'd hate for her to take a pay cut.

I dropped Clementine off and made my way to the inn

with my thoughts swirling. The only chance I had right now was to make sure that my conversation with Penny went my way. If I wanted to stay in this town that was rapidly becoming my home, I needed to find the best way to pitch it to Penny.

She wasn't concerned with feelings or emotions. I needed to hit her with facts and numbers if I wanted to win her over.

When I got to the inn, I parked and managed to carry all the shoeboxes into the house in one trip. Once they were dumped in the living room—where we were going to host the book club—I set out to find Archer. All the lights were on, and I'd seen his truck in the parking lot.

I found him in an upstairs bathroom, grouting the newly replaced tile in the shower. The sleeves of his t-shirt were tucked up at his shoulders. He wore a backwards baseball cap, and grout smudged his arms and left a tiny streak across his cheek. He was humming to the Johnny Cash song that was blaring from his phone.

I leaned against the doorframe and watched him. He was mesmerizing. The way he moved. His arm muscles rippled as he swiped his arm back and forth on the walls. My lips tipped up into a smile as the resolve to convince Penny to let me stay coursed through me.

It didn't take long for Archer to realize that I was there. He did a double take before his gaze settled on me and he dropped his arms. After setting the grout float and container down, he straightened.

"How long have you been there?" he asked as he stepped out of the tub.

I shrugged as he approached. My heart pounded in my chest as I reveled in his closeness. He laughed as he moved to wash his hands.

He turned, resting one hand on the wall, and leaned in closer to me. I kept my gaze trained on him, not breaking the connection that was zinging through us. He leaned down and brushed his lips against mine, before trailing kisses down my chin and settling on my neck.

"How was shopping with Clem?" he murmured against my skin.

I smiled. "It was great. We talked about everything." I furrowed my brow as I thought about mentioning Penny and the uncertainty of what was happening in the future. I pushed that thought out. I didn't want to cause him concern when there didn't need to be any.

Archer pulled back and blinked a few times as he studied me. It felt as if he was waiting for me to expand on my response, but I just shrugged. "Girl stuff."

He wrinkled his nose as he pulled back and shoved his hands into the front pockets of his jeans. "What do you think about the new tiles?"

I glanced over his shoulder and smiled at the white subway tiles he'd just installed. "They look great."

"I'm sorry I couldn't salvage the originals, but these will hold up much better." He moved to stand behind me and wrap his arms around my waist. I leaned back, breathing in deeply and savoring the feeling that came from being this close to him.

My life seemed absolutely perfect, and yet, in a few short days, all of it could be pulled out from underneath me.

I swallowed as fear built up inside of me. I wasn't going to think like that right now.

For now, I was going to put to bed all the thoughts of the future and live.

I'd worry about what I was going to say later.

CLEMENTINE

I was a jumble of nerves as I climbed into my car the next day and headed to the inn to get ready. I'd packed my back seat full of food, which was a happy distraction, but now things were getting real.

People were coming to the book club—people who might not have the greatest opinion of me—and were going to sit in a room with me and Maggie. Even though I knew these people, the thought of hosting a party had my nerves out of whack.

Thankfully, Maggie was all smiles when I pulled into the parking lot and turned off the engine. She'd been standing next to Archer's truck, talking to him. At first glance, it had looked as if they were standing a little too close together, but as soon as I climbed out of my car, they'd stepped apart.

Maggie came over to talk to me.

"Good morning," she sang out. The wind picked up her

skirt and swung it around. Her hair was curled and bounced when she walked.

"You look amazing," I said as I pulled open the back door. Maggie reached in to retrieve some of the containers back there.

"Thanks," Maggie said. "You look great too."

I blew the chunk of hair out of my face that had wiggled loose from my bun. I wished what she said was true. With the sweat from my nerves and running around all morning, I felt as salty as the sea. "I feel like a mess," I said as I retrieved the other items that Maggie couldn't carry.

We walked side by side toward the inn. Archer approached with a bag of cement on his shoulder. I studied him, and he shrugged.

"I'm working on the back patio," he said as he veered off to the left and disappeared around the house.

I glanced over at Maggie, who was watching him. "Are things working out with my brother?" I asked.

Maggie startled, whipping her gaze back to me. It might have been my imagination, but it seemed as if her cheeks flushed. I raised my eyebrows, but she just laughed it off.

"Oh, yeah. Archer's great. It's probably why the inn looks as good as it does. He's a hard worker...er, they all are."

Her words poured out of her, and for a moment, I wondered if something was going on that I didn't know about. Why was she acting like this?

We were in the kitchen now, laying out the containers onto the counter. I didn't have time to think about Maggie's strange reaction as I began to lay the food out onto platters.

The furniture that Maggie ordered had been delivered, and it looked as if she had been hard at work all morning arranging the pieces in the living room. A large dark-blue couch ran along one side of the room. On the other side, a tall buffet sat with a bouquet of flowers tucked inside of a vase.

Maggie had painted the walls a soft grey, and with the sunlight streaming into the room, it made the atmosphere calm and peaceful. I took in a deep breath as my anxiety stilled. I could do this. The book club would be a success. It would be something that the women of Magnolia would talk about for years to come.

We laid the food out on the buffet and set up a small drink station at the mini bar. Then we situated the stilettos at the door, so when people came in, they could easily grab theirs. We giggled when Maggie said it felt like we were channeling our true Korean selves—where they take off their shoes and wear slippers in the house.

By the time we were finished, we collapsed on the couch and stretched our legs out in front of us.

"Ready?" Maggie asked.

I smiled and nodded. "Ready."

Shari was the first to show. I saw her pull into the small parking lot, and I hurried over to the door and threw it open before she had time to knock. "Good morning," I sang out with a smile.

Shari looked startled for a moment before her expression morphed into a smile. "Good morning."

I stepped to the side so that she could enter. I showed her where her stilettos were, and she gave me her *seriously* look before slipping them on. I wasn't a high heel wearer either, so I kept my lips pinched when she stumbled a few times as she made her way into the living room. After all, I wasn't doing much better.

I introduced her to Maggie, and they chatted while Shari filled up her plate with food. I made my way back over to the door when I heard three solid knocks. I didn't have to open it to know who was on the other side. Victoria had a knock that matched her personality. Sharp and abrupt.

I opened the door, and Victoria ran her gaze over me. Her bright red hair was pulled back into a french braid, and her gaze was skeptical as she studied me and then the room. I invited her in, and she didn't waste any time barreling forward. I thought about getting her shoes for her, but she was opening them before I could say anything.

Not wanting to get into anything with her, I left her alone in the foyer and made my way over to where Maggie and Shari were talking.

"Really?" Maggie asked, her eyebrows rising.

Shari was nodding, and I became intrigued with what they were talking about.

"What's up?" I asked.

Shari flicked her gaze over to me before she stuffed a mini eclair into her mouth. "Jake just texted me."

The entire room faded away as I turned to focus my attention on Shari. Maybe it had been the shock of hearing his name after such a long time. Or the fact that Shari had said it in a cautious manner. As if she were worried about my reaction.

Brushing off the initial surge of drunken butterflies in my stomach, I furrowed my brow and shrugged. "Really? What did he say?"

I could feel Shari's scrutiny as she studied me. But thankfully, she must have decided that this wasn't the time or place to bring up our past and explained to Maggie and me that he was coming home.

My ears rang, and I felt as if I were going to vomit as she continued talking. My life had changed so much in such a short period of time, that inviting Jake back home —back into my life—wasn't a change I was prepared to make.

I swallowed as Maggie asked questions about Jake— ones that I already knew the answers to—and made my way to the door to invite a short, dark-haired girl into the inn. She had bright blue eyes and looked like she was in her twenties.

"Hi," she said cautiously as she glanced inside the inn. "My mom sent me here. I'm Fiona."

I reached out my hand. "Ah, you're Anna's daughter.

I'm Clementine." I stepped to the side so she could enter. "Welcome to Magnolia Inn."

She smiled shyly, and I helped her locate her shoes. Then I brought her into the living room where I introduced her to the other women. Victoria didn't miss a beat as she crossed the room and started talking to Fiona. A few more Magnolia women arrived, and I was busy playing hostess as I greeted them and handed them their shoes.

When it seemed as if everyone who was going to come had arrived, Maggie and I called to order the first session of our book club. Our main goal was to introduce everyone to each other and pick a book. It seemed as if we had a great group of women. They chatted and laughed as they ate.

The two hours we'd allotted for the meeting flew by fast, and even though Victoria was there in her *I'm better than everyone* attitude, I was enjoying myself. For a moment, I even forgot that when I got home, I would return to an empty house.

Just as we wrapped up the meeting, there was a knock on the door. I glanced over at Maggie, who looked confused as she met my gaze. I wondered who'd decided to show up so late. I watched as Maggie disappeared into the foyer to get the door.

"So we are planning on meeting next month to discuss *Where the Crawdads Sing*," I said to the ladies. They all nodded and stood. Most walked elegantly around the room. They seemed to have experience with stilettos and rugs. The rest of us looked like fawns just learning to stand. I was one of them.

Voices from the foyer drew my attention, and an elegant woman entered the room. Her grey hair was pulled back into a bun and she had a multicolored scarf wrapped around her neck and tucked into her dark blue suit jacket.

She was pulling a suitcase behind her, and her heels clicked on the hardwood. Her gaze swept across all of us, and then she turned to focus on Maggie. "What's going on here?" she asked.

Maggie's confident demeanor had slipped. She was standing with her shoulders slumped. Her right arm was folded across her stomach and she was holding onto her left elbow. I studied her expression, confused as to what would have her acting like this.

"We're reviving a book club," Maggie said, her voice was low and hushed.

The woman stared at Maggie, and then a moment later, turned her attention back to the room. "Penny Brown," she said as she nodded toward us.

Brown? Was this Maggie's mom?

"Clementine," I said as I stepped forward. Just as I did, the heel of my shoe caught on the rug and I pitched forward. Thankfully, I caught myself before I rammed into Penny.

I could feel Penny's stare on me as she took a step back. She adjusted the strap of her purse higher up onto her shoulder and cleared her throat. "It's nice to meet you," she said.

Silence filled the room. The Magnolia residents were watching what this newcomer was going to do. Wanting to defuse the tension, I let out a laugh and nodded toward the ladies.

"I guess that's a wrap," I said as I reached down and slipped off my heels.

I could feel the relief flood the room as everyone swarmed past Maggie and Penny as they slipped off their heels, put on the shoes they came with, and headed out the front door. I busied myself with cleaning up the now empty platters of food, while keeping part of my focus on Maggie and her mom.

"So this is what you've been doing?" Penny asked as she abandoned her suitcase and began to walk around the room.

I felt bad for the furniture, walls, and floor. I felt like I was going to melt under Penny's scrutiny. And, with the way she was studying the elements around her, I half expected the entire room to erupt into flames.

"I found a picture of Grandma..." Maggie started, but when Penny snapped her gaze up to meet hers, Maggie's voice faded away.

Penny stared for a moment before she blew out her breath. "Our agreement was that you would fix up the inn so I could sell it." Penny reached up, removed her glasses that she had perched on her nose, and began to rub her temples. "Not rekindle the past."

I shuffled off to the kitchen with the food platters in hand. Just as I slipped from the room, I heard Maggie say, "I thought it was a good idea."

I hurried to set the platters down next to the sink and hid next to the doorway so I could listen in. Penny was saying that if she'd wanted to resurrect her mother's past, she would have done so herself.

The back door opened, and Archer came strolling in, whistling. He was dusty—no doubt from the cement. I hurried to raise my finger to my lips. His noisy entrance overwhelmed the voices from the living room.

Archer raised his eyebrows as he tiptoed over to me. He stood behind me, leaning in toward the door. "What are we listening to?" he asked.

I elbowed him. He let out a deep humph, but thankfully, he remained quiet.

"Well, I was thinking that I...could stay here and run the inn," Maggie's voice had lost her confident edge. Suddenly the realization that she might have to sell the inn and move off the island sank in around me.

"Who's Maggie talking to?" I was startled by the depth to Archer's voice. It was strange that he sounded as worried as I felt.

I glanced behind me to see that Archer's expression had fallen. His playful demeanor that I was beginning to get used to had faded.

"Her mom. She's not happy," I whispered.

Archer didn't speak further, which led me to believe that he already knew of her impending visit. It seemed as if he and Maggie were closer than I thought. I made a mental note to ask him more about that later.

"That wasn't the plan, Margaret. I make plans, and I stick to them. Running Magnolia Inn is not something I want to do. Selling is the only thing I plan on doing with this place." Penny's sigh was loud, and I could feel her annoyance in it. "If you're willing to buy, I can sell to you, but we both know that's not an option. Neither is holding onto a property full of bad memories. I'm ready to move forward."

I waited for Maggie to respond. I waited for her to tell her mom how much Magnolia meant to her. That selling and leaving would leave a giant hole in a community that was getting used to her being around. That it would dampen the hope that had sparked with the idea of Magnolia Inn reopening.

"I don't say this to be mean. I think it's time we move off this island and move on with our lives." Penny's voice was strained, and I took comfort in the fact that she sounded more human than not.

"I understand," Maggie said.

I glanced behind me at Archer to see his clenched jaw muscles. He was working through something, and I was beginning to realize just how much Magnolia Inn—and in turn, Maggie—meant to him. His gaze darkened as he pushed away from the doorframe.

He shoved his hands through his hair as he walked over to the fridge and pulled out a bottle of water. I could feel his anger as he twisted off the cap and downed half the liquid in a single swallow.

I furrowed my brow as I watched him, but before I could say anything, the sound of footsteps approaching caused my entire body to stiffen. I watched as Penny and Maggie walked into the kitchen. Maggie was quiet as she kept her gaze trained on Penny.

"What's the ETA for completion?" she asked.

Maggie cleared her throat as I saw her gaze drift over to Archer, whose relaxed demeanor had disappeared and all that remained was a flat stare. It was his defense mechanism. I'd recognize it anywhere.

"I would say about two weeks," Archer said as he stepped forward, setting his water bottle down on the counter next to him.

Penny's gaze drifted over to him, and I watched as her gaze raked over him. "And you are?"

"This is Archer...the guy I hired to help," Maggie said, her voice drifting to a whisper with each word.

Archer's gaze flicked down to her, and I saw the hurt that flashed in it. Something was definitely going on between them. A feeling of betrayal surged through me. Not from the fact that my friend and my brother had started something up—if she wasn't currently talking about leaving the island, I would have been thrilled—but from the fact that she'd kept it from me for so long.

There were moments when she could have told me. But she'd chosen not to. That hurt and made me wonder why.

Penny studied Archer for a moment longer before she sighed and glanced back over at Maggie. "Can we have a moment? Alone?"

Maggie's cheeks reddened as she held her mom's gaze and then shot me a pleading look. "Do you guys mind?"

I wasn't going to stick around where I wasn't welcome, and Archer looked like he felt the same. He was out of the kitchen before anyone could say anything further. I could see the disappointment and fear in his expression and gait. For someone who went through as much trauma as he had, I could only imagine what was going through his mind right now.

Especially if he and Maggie had started something.

I nodded over at Penny and shot Maggie one last glance before I slipped out of the kitchen, over to my shoes, and then out the front door. Archer's truck was pulling out of the parking lot as I climbed into my car. I contemplated following after him just to get the details but decided against it.

He didn't look like he was in the mood to speak to anyone. And right now, the last thing I wanted was to be on the receiving end of his backlash.

The drive home was confusing. I walked into my empty house and threw my keys on the side table and collapsed on the couch. I stared around me, and the realization of just how lonely I was washed over me.

I stifled a sob as I forced my tears back. I wasn't going to cry anymore. I was tired of feeling bad for myself. I was ready to face my future, whatever it looked like.

I really wanted Maggie to be a part of that. We'd grown close over the last few months, and the thought of her leaving left me with a hollow feeling in my chest. But I wasn't going to let it get me down.

Regardless of what Maggie did, I was going to need to face my new normal head on. I needed to find myself sans Dad, Archer, and Maggie.

I needed to discover what I loved, and I needed to start right now.

20

MAGGIE

My entire body felt as if a hundred-pound weight was resting on my shoulders. Penny was here, and Archer and Clementine had stormed out. They weren't just obeying Penny's desire to be alone—they were angry. Which was understandable.

Especially when it came to Archer. I saw the look on his face when I introduced him to Penny. His once cheerful demeanor dropped, and he didn't look back as he left the room. Clementine looked equally confused but less angry. I hoped I would be able to explain myself to her in time.

Right now, I needed to tackle the mess I'd made and there was only one way of doing that—facing Penny.

She was wandering around the kitchen, opening cupboards, and checking the appliances. I could tell she was assessing the items there. I watched her, wondering what she was thinking.

"The kitchen is adequate," she said as she ran her finger along the white marble countertop.

"Archer did a great job," I said as I folded my arms and gave her my most intense stare. I wanted her to know that I knew what I was doing. Hiring Archer and his crew was one of the best decisions I'd made here on the island.

Penny studied me. "Archer…" she said slowly and allowed her voice to drift off. There was so much implied in that one word, and it angered me.

"Yes, Archer. He's a great guy. I'm—" I wanted to be honest. I wanted to talk with my own mother about the guys in my life, but there was a part of me that was holding back. I didn't want to confess too much too soon. After all, could I trust her with my feelings? There was a greater likelihood that she would hurt me than not.

Penny raised her eyebrows. "You're what?"

I sighed and turned so that her stare was less penetrating. "I'm grateful he's in my life," I said.

When Penny didn't respond, I turned to see that she was leaning against the counter with her arms folded. She was tapping her fingers against her bicep and surveying the room. Her gaze finally landed on me.

"You're angry," she said.

I stared at her. Was she serious? "Yes, I'm angry," I said. I wanted to speak more. I wanted to tell her how I really felt, but I couldn't bring myself to do it. There was a part of me that was holding back, and I was beginning to realize that it was that part that had angered Clementine and Archer.

Penny sighed as she loosened the scarf around her neck. "Why are you angry?"

I felt like an indignant child, standing there glaring at my mother. Maybe there was some truth to my immaturity. After all, it wasn't like we'd had the normal mother-daughter relationship. She was out of my life for so long that I'd never really rebelled against her.

Was this a stage I was going to have to go through in order to move forward?

I sighed, releasing some of the pent-up anger I felt. I relaxed my shoulders. Even though I felt frustrated, I knew that releasing all of that anger on her wasn't productive. If I wanted her to do something for me, lashing out was the last thing I should do.

"I guess I was just hoping we could have a discussion about the inn instead of you just dictating what was going to happen," I said in the calmest voice I could muster.

Penny's eyebrows went up, and I could see her chew on my comment. She studied me and then blew out her breath as she glanced around. "Okay, let's talk."

I blinked a few times. I hadn't expected her to be so open. This was definitely not her usual personality. "Really?" I asked before I could stop myself.

Penny chuckled. "Is that not what you want?"

"No, it's what I want," I said quickly. The last thing I wanted was for her to back down from being open. I gathered my thoughts and then started.

"The inn means so much to so many people here in Magnolia," I said. Emotions rose up inside me as I thought about all the people I'd become friends with in the short amount of time I'd been here. Everyone meant so much to me, and the idea of walking out on them hurt me inside.

"It can stay open. I can make it a stipulation that the owner run it as it was intended to be run," Penny responded.

I swallowed. "It means a lot to me," I whispered.

Penny's eyebrows rose. "Why?"

I reached out and rested my hand on the wall next to me. I'd never felt so close to a building as I did to this place. It not only had to do with the fact that Clementine felt like a sister and Archer felt like...so much more. It was the fact that, for once in my life, I felt like I belonged.

"I feel like this is where I need to be," I whispered.

From the corner of my eye, I could see Penny studying me. Her expression was one that was hard to read. I was thankful that she was taking a moment to respond and that she wasn't just pushing my feelings aside.

I swallowed as I glanced at her. "What happened with you and Grandma?" I asked. I held my breath as I waited for her to respond.

Penny paused before she wandered over to the fridge and pulled out a water bottle. She twisted the cap off and took a drink. A few moments later, she sighed and set her bottle down on the countertop. "Things with your grandmother were never easy. Dorthy liked her life here on Magnolia Island. When your grandfather's mother got sick, he decided to move our family from here." Penny's voice was soft and hurt. It was something I'd never heard before. It was startling, hearing her be vulnerable like this.

I kept my lips pinched together and allowed her to continue.

"Your grandmother wouldn't leave. She said this was her life, and if your grandfather wanted to go, then he could...without her." Penny rubbed her temples as she closed her eyes. "Our family broke apart. I went to live with your grandfather, and Dorthy...she remained here."

I studied her. So much of my personal life was exactly like what she was describing. Tears pricked my eyes as I realized how broken my own mother was. She had to make the same decision I did. Is that why she never fought me about staying with Dad? Because she knew the pain something like that brought to one's soul?

Penny was quiet as she stared out the window. She had a far-off look in her eyes as she took in a deep breath. "Magnolia has always been a source of pain for me. So the idea of keeping the inn—of coming here—is almost too much to bear."

That I understood. I could only imagine what I was asking of my mother. The pain that she was carrying because of her mother's decisions had to hurt. But I had to believe that there was a way to forgive and move on. I'd never wanted something like that more than I did right then.

"It doesn't have to be like that," I whispered.

Penny glanced over. Her brow was knit together as she studied me. "What?"

I realized that I was talking more about our relationship than her relationship with her mother. Theirs was one that couldn't move forward. Ours could.

"I'm sorry," I said. Tears began to slip down my cheeks as I offered her a soft smile. I wanted so badly to move on from this, and I was beginning to realize that it had to start with me. "I'm sorry for picking Dad over you."

Penny's expression fell as she stared at me. I could see tears as they gathered on her eyelids. Seeing this reaction told me everything I needed to know. She had been hurt. All of her facade of strength had been built to hide her hurt. A normal human reaction.

"I never blamed you," she whispered as she hastily raised her hand up to her cheek to wipe away the tear that had slid down.

"I know. But it hurt. And I'm sorry," I said as I crossed the room and wrapped her into a hug.

At first, Penny stiffened. But then she began to relax and even returned the hug. It was strange, being this close to her—being this vulnerable—but it felt right. If I was going to move on from the mess that was my past, I needed to start with fixing the relationships in my life that were broken.

No matter the result, I wanted a better relationship with my mother.

A few moments later, I pulled back and offered her a smile. Penny's demeanor changed as she smiled back at me. Even though our relationship was still broken, we were making strides to fix it, and for now, that was all I could ask for.

I reached over and pulled out a tissue. I handed it to her and took one for myself. I dabbed at my eyes and cleared my throat. "If you want to sell the inn, I under- stand. But I wish that you would take a few days to think about it. The inn could not only serve as a stream of income, but it could help you move on from your rela- tionship with Dorthy," I said, offering her a smile.

Penny studied me and then sighed as she wiped her cheeks. Her shoulders slumped, and she nodded as she glanced down and fiddled with the tissue. "I'll think about it," she said.

I patted her shoulder. "Let's get you a room, and you can settle in."

Penny nodded. "I'd like that."

I brought her up to the second floor and into one of the rooms that I'd finished decorating. I was still in the process of filling all the rooms with furniture. Since we weren't sure what we were going to do with the inn, I'd been careful to only fill a few of them—to give the future buyers an idea of what the inn would look like.

Penny was grateful and gave me a smile as she shut the door. I spent the next hour cleaning up from the book club meeting. When I went to check on her, I found Penny asleep on the bed.

Not wanting to disturb her, I left her alone. Once the kitchen was clean and the living room floor swept and mopped, I found my phone and texted Clementine. While

I waited, I decided to focus on painting the laundry room in the back. It was a dark room, so I was painting the walls a light grey to bring in more light.

I needed something to distract me from worrying about the lack of response from Clementine. I really hoped I hadn't ruined our relationship. I knew she wanted me to fight for the inn, and the fact that I didn't respond the way she wanted me to had to hurt.

She'd just lost her dad, and I was sure that the prospect of me leaving wasn't something she wanted to deal with right now. I needed to assure her that, no matter what happened with the inn, we were still going to be friends.

Fifteen minutes into painting, my phone chimed. I hurried to set my roller down and wipe my hands before I picked it up. Relief washed over me when I saw that it was a text from Clementine.

How are things with your mom?

I moved to sit on the stool I'd just been standing on. I blew a strand of hair from my face as I texted her back.

Hard. She's struggling with a lot right now. Apparently she and my grandmother had some issues. Being at the inn just brings them back.

I waited for her to respond. Thankfully, this time, it didn't take as long.

I'm sorry. And I'm sorry for leaving so fast like we did.

I smiled as I read her response. I was grateful that she didn't seem mad at me. I knew she wanted me to fight for the inn, but I felt as if I were stuck back in the same place I'd been when I had to decide between

Dad or Penny. Deciding between the inn and Penny felt just as hard. There wasn't anything I wanted more than to come out of this unscathed in either area.

No worries. It gave me more time to talk to Penny. I'm working with her, and she seems to have softened to the idea. But I need to wait for her to make the decision on her own. I can't force her.

A weight was slowly lifting off my shoulders with each word I texted. For so long, I'd carried the guilt of picking Dad. Yet, allowing my mom time to make her decision felt as if I were making up for the fact that I'd left. I couldn't just push her for something I wanted, like fixing our broken relationship. I just had to believe that she would come around on her own.

That she would see how good the inn was for me—and for her.

I understand. I just wish it meant you were sticking around instead of leaving.

I nodded. I was the same.

She'll come around. I'm sure of it. But pushing her isn't the answer.

It took a little bit longer before Clementine responded. Her answer made me smile.

I was the same with Dad, so I can't fault her for needing to take her time. Wanna do dinner tonight? We could go out with your mom.

My heart swelled with appreciation for my new best friend. Clementine was sweet and kind and exactly what I needed in a friend. I was grateful to have her around me while I went through this.

Definitely.

I paused as I stared at the keyboard on my phone. I wanted to ask her about Archer, but I wasn't sure how. Then, I brushed aside my fear and typed what I wanted to ask.

Is Archer okay?

I sent the message before I chickened out.

I haven't seen him since he left.

My stomach sank as I read those words. Where would he have gone? Was he mad at me? I still couldn't forget the look in his eye as he walked out of the kitchen earlier. It broke my heart.

My phone chimed, and I glanced down to read Clementine's text.

Is there something going on between the two of you?

I studied her question. Wondering myself how to classify our relationship. I wanted to say yes. Archer meant a lot more to me than I'd even imagined I could feel again. But with our current status, I wasn't sure what he wanted. Or if he wanted anyone to know, especially his sister.

We can talk about it during dinner.

Clementine sent a thumbs-up emoji along with, *Sounds good. 7 at Shakes?*

Yep.

I stared at my screen as I clicked on Archer's name. My finger hovered over the text button. I wanted to message him to see how he was doing. I was pretty sure he wanted to know what Penny was doing with the inn, and I didn't think he was going to be satisfied with "I don't know." If he was hurting, that kind of response would be like pouring salt in the wound.

Hurting him was the last thing I wanted to do.

Letting out a deep sigh, I found my music app and turned on my favorites. As the music filled the air, I pushed aside all of my fear and picked up the paint roller. I was going to lose myself in painting.

My hope was that I would get the work done that I needed, while forgetting how much pain was coursing through me right now.

If these were my last days here on Magnolia Island, I was going to make them worth it. After all, I was going to leave a different person. A stronger, happier person.

That was one gift this place gave me, and regressing because of my frustration felt as if I was spitting in the face of the people and place that had given me so much.

I was a changed person, and I was going to continue to be. No matter what.

21

CLEMENTINE

My determination to discover who I was now waned, and instead of getting on the computer and taking a personality test to tell me my dream job, I found myself lost in a K-drama. Whatever my problems were, they would still be there tomorrow.

But today, enjoying the bucket of ice cream in the freezer and the mushy romance of my favorite show felt like the best decision I could make.

I was curled up on the couch with my feet tucked up under me and a blanket wrapped around me when the door opened and Archer appeared. His hair was disheveled, and his expression soured as he kicked his shoes off and slammed the door.

I parted my lips, but he didn't wait for me to speak. Instead he marched over to the fridge and pulled it open. I heard the crack of a tab and watched as he tipped his head back and downed one of the Cokes I'd put in there this morning.

He was angry. I could feel it in the energy around him.

Fed up with his moody, teenage behavior, I threw off my blanket and stood. I walked over to him with my hands on my hips. It took him a moment to acknowledge me. He dropped his gaze to me for a brief moment before he moved to step around me.

I was too quick and cut off his retreat.

He tried to move again, but I anticipated it and hurried to stand in front of him.

Archer growled as he picked me up and set me down behind him. I squirmed to fight him, but he was too quick and too strong for me to do anything.

"Archer," I yelled as I hurried to get back in front of him, but he quickened his pace. He was inside of his room before I could stop him. Thankfully, I got to his door-frame before he could slam the door. He glared as he tried to move me, but I fought back.

Finally, he sighed and left me alone as he wandered over to his bed and flopped down. He covered his eyes with his elbow. "Go away, Clem," he growled.

I folded my arms and shook my head. I was done with going away. I'd spent too long staying out of his life, and I was angry at myself for letting him spiral. I was deter-mined not to do that again. He was gearing up for the loss of Maggie, and I could sense his desire to fold in on himself again.

"No," I said, firmly. I wasn't going to be pushed around anymore. I needed Archer more than anything right now. He had to know that. Now that Dad was gone, I would be completely alone if Maggie left. He had to step up and be the older brother I needed.

When he didn't respond, I hurried over to his bed and sat down next to him. I waited for his response, but none came. Instead, his breathing deepened, and for a moment, I was worried that he'd fallen asleep.

"Archer?" I asked as I reached out and shoved his shoulder.

"What?" he asked. His voice was low and resigned. I could hear the pain in his voice as much as I could see it in his body language.

And I hated it. I hated that my brother had gone through so much pain in his life. If I could, I would do anything to take it away. He deserved so much more than what the world had dealt to him.

I thought his job with Maggie was helping him see that. But now, I was beginning to see that it was Maggie herself that was changing him.

"Are you dating Maggie?" I asked. I needed to know if I was going to help him.

Archer remained still. I knew my brother well enough to know that he was chewing on my question. Honestly, I didn't need him to respond. I knew the answer just from his body language.

"Don't be mad at her," I said. "She's trying. Her relationship with her mom is...complicated."

Archer sighed as he dropped his arm from his face and moved to sit so his back was resting against his headboard. He ran his gaze over me and then scoffed as he tipped his head back and closed his eyes.

"Is it that obvious?"

I chuckled. "A little. I haven't seen you care so much about something since…" I stopped myself as I studied him. I didn't want to bring up Elise, but somehow, my mouth had run off and done it anyway.

Archer tipped his head forward and opened his eyes. He studied me for a moment as he took in a deep breath. "Ever since Elise?" he asked.

Tears filled my eyes as the pain of losing my niece filled my soul. I hated that she had to die. I hated that she was taken from the perfect father. Archer loved her more than anything. He really was the best dad.

"Yes," I whispered as a tear slipped down my cheek.

Archer reached forward and caught the tear with his fingertips. Then he smiled at me. It wasn't his carefree one, but one that said, *I understand*. We were both hurting and struggling with what to do with the pain.

"I know, and I'm sorry. I'm sorry that I left you alone. I shouldn't have." He reached down and grabbed my hand. After giving it a quick squeeze, he patted it with his free hand as he glanced around.

I studied him, noting the tears that had formed on his lids as well. "You were hurting. I couldn't hold that against you."

Archer glanced back up at me. "It's not an excuse. You needed me, and I wasn't here."

I shrugged. "You came around eventually."

He studied me, and then a soft smile spread across his lips. "You're the best little sister, you know that? I couldn't have asked for a better one."

I nodded and flicked my hair from my shoulder. "Yeah, I know. You're lucky to have me."

He chuckled. "I am. I don't deserve the women who grace me with their love and patience."

I reached forward and pulled my brother into a hug. "You do. You just don't see it."

He hugged me tight and then pulled back. "Then I'm lucky that you see all of that in your broken brother."

I laughed as I smiled up at him. "Of course. You're stuck with me. We've been together for this long; it would be stupid of me to walk away now."

Archer's chuckle died down as he studied me. "You're really okay with Maggie and me?"

I met his gaze. "As long as you don't hurt her, I am. She's great. You're great. It only makes sense that two great people find each other."

He dropped his gaze as he nodded. "What if she leaves?" he asked.

I reached down and patted his hands. "I have faith that she'll stay. She's working through things with her mom, but I promise you, she doesn't want to go."

He sighed and nodded. Then he moved to swing his

legs to the side of his bed and stand. He crossed the room and picked up his phone. I stood and pulled it from him before he could text her. "Wait. We're meeting for dinner tonight, and you can talk to her then."

He glanced down at his watch. "What time?"

"Seven. Do you think you can wait until then?"

Archer growled and then smiled as he nodded. "I think I can wait an hour." Then he glanced around the room. "I'm going to shower and get ready."

"Ah, Prince Charming is getting ready to go after his princess?"

Archer threw me an annoyed glance, but when he turned, I saw the smile that emerged. My heart felt happy as I watched my brother shut the bathroom door and heard the pipes squeak on.

I hadn't seen him this happy—this hopeful—in a long time.

I wandered into my room and changed into a pair of jeans and a t-shirt. I didn't have to impress anyone right now, unlike Archer. Who, from the cloud of his cologne, was hoping that his smell alone would win Maggie back.

I just wanted to talk to Mrs. Brown to let her know how much the inn meant to this island and how much Maggie meant to the residents. Hopefully, she'd be open to hearing from me, and, fingers crossed, she'd be willing to change her mind.

———

I followed behind Archer as we walked into Shakes at seven on the dot. I glanced around but didn't see Maggie or her mom. Brenda greeted us and sat us at a booth in the corner.

Archer was wearing dark jeans and a light-green button-up shirt. His hair was styled, and he looked handsome—albeit nervous. He kept wiping his hands on his jeans and shifting in his seat.

"Dude," I whispered, having had enough of his leg and arm bumping mine.

"Sorry," he mumbled. "I'm nervous."

I studied him as a sly smile spread across my lips. I yelped as a finger jabbed into my side. I glared at him, but from the desperate look in his eye, he wasn't in the mood to be teased. He was nervous, so I decided to play nice.

"Relax. She cares about you too. She asked how you were doing."

He paused. "She did?" he asked as he stared me down.

"Yes, now would you like me to pass her a note during PE?"

He glared at me, but before he could say anything, the door opened and the bells jingled. We both turned to see Maggie and her mom walk in. Archer instantly stiffened.

My poor brother. I would be surprised if he made it out of this alive.

"Maggie!" I called out as I rose up slightly and raised my hand.

She glanced over and smiled at me, but as soon as her gaze shifted to Archer, her expression fell. Penny didn't seem to notice her change in demeanor. Instead, she stared at me for a moment before she nodded and walked over with Maggie trailing behind her.

"It's good to see you again, Mrs. Brown," I said as Maggie sat and scooted until she was across from me. Penny sat next to her. I could tell she was used to eating in restaurants that had five stars instead of the five ketchup bottles that the local Magnolia Sun gave out.

Brenda made her way to our table, took our drink orders, and then left us alone to look at the menu.

The tension at the table was high. I could tell that Archer and Maggie were trying not to look at each other but failing horribly at it. I wanted to demand that the two of them take it outside and make up, but I didn't want to draw attention to their relationship in case Penny didn't know.

We kept our conversion light after we ordered. Then the table fell silent once our food was delivered. By the time our plates were cleared, I was pretty certain I was going to go insane from all the small talk. Archer and Maggie needed to work through their stuff, and I needed to work on Mrs. Brown.

"Would you like to take a walk on the beach?" I asked as we all scooted from the booth and stood.

Mrs. Brown may not have realized that I was talking to her until I grabbed her elbow to keep her from walking away.

She startled as she whipped her gaze over to me. "Were

you talking to me?" she asked as she pressed her hand to her chest.

I nodded.

She glanced over at Maggie, who was staring at Archer, and then sighed. "Sure. Why not."

That wasn't the ringing endorsement that I wanted, but I'd take it. We left Maggie and Archer standing awkwardly next to each other as we slipped out of the restaurant and across the street. We walked through the sand as we approached the water's edge. The sun was beginning to set, and the sky looked as if it were on fire.

I slipped off my shoes, and Penny did the same as we began walking down the beach. There was so much I wanted to ask Penny—so much I wanted to convince her of—but I wasn't sure how to do it.

"How long have you lived in Magnolia?" Penny asked. The fact that she broke the silence first threw me off for a moment.

I glanced over at her and then back down at the waves that were washing over my feet. "Basically my whole life. My adoptive parents are Janet and Dirk Ramsey."

Her expression grew contemplative. "I've heard that name," she said.

"They ran Magnolia Hardware. My mom was friends with Dorthy." I eyed her. Even though I didn't remember Penny, I remembered Dorthy. I was young when she left, so the memory was cloudy, but if I tried, I could picture my mother sitting at the table playing cribbage with a woman with pure white hair and an infectious laugh.

I hated how faded my memories of my mother had become. I wish I'd spent more time with her. I was a moody teenager when she passed away, and I spent a good portion of the time I could have spent with her, away.

"Ah, yes, I remember Janet and Dirk." She glanced over at me. "How are they?"

I sighed as I kicked some sand. "Mom passed away, and I just had to put Dad in a home." Tears pricked my eyes as I thought about my decision. "Alzheimer's."

"I'm so sorry," Penny said, her voice hushed.

I swallowed. "It's okay. Time marches on." That was a truth I was beginning to understand. No matter what I did. No matter how much I wanted to stop the flow of time, I would never be successful. Time was a fact of life, and you could either spend your effort fighting it or you could lean into it, making sure each moment is a momentous one.

"That's the truth," Penny said. Her voice had turned reverent, and it intrigued me. I glanced up to see that her expression had softened.

"I get why you want to sell Magnolia. I have enough bad memories on this island to make any sane person want to run away screaming." I tucked my hair behind my ear as the wind picked up and caused it to dance around my face. "But there's something to be said about the magic of this place."

Penny remained quiet as we continued walking. It took a few moments before I heard her take in a deep breath. "Mom always said there was a magic to Magnolia. One that could never be replicated anywhere else.

I nodded. "It's true. Magnolia is a magical place."

We walked in silence. We both seemed distracted by our own memories. The waves crashed around us, and a sense of peace filled my chest. Penny wasn't out to get Maggie. She was a woman who was struggling with her past, just like the rest of us.

I couldn't fault her for that. I just wished she could see how much Magnolia meant to Maggie and how much having Maggie here meant to us.

We turned around a few minutes later and headed back to the restaurant. We looked for Maggie and Archer, but when we couldn't find them, I glanced over at Penny and asked if she wanted a cup of coffee.

She looked tired but agreed. We walked over to The Hideout and sat down. I sent a quick text to Maggie to let her know where we were as our drinks were delivered by Fiona. Anna stopped by our table, and she and Penny started talking. They laughed and reminisced. Apparently, they'd gone to high school together.

I sat back with my arms folded and watched the world around me as it moved. Sure, life moved at a slower pace here than most places, and we were a simple community, but when I really thought about it, this was my home.

I'd complained about being stuck here. About feeling as if I could never really move forward. But in the quiet of nights such as this, I realized that fact was far from the truth.

I loved Magnolia, and when I thought about leaving, a feeling of dread washed over me. The old Clementine, the one who'd wanted to leave, wasn't who I was anymore. I was an older, more experienced Clementine. And this Clementine?

Well, she wanted to stay.

This was her home.

And I was never going to leave.

22

MAGGIE

Archer was quiet as we walked side by side. The water washed over my feet, and I reveled in the shock of that sensation mixed with the warmth that spread across my skin. I had my arms folded, but every so often, Archer brushed against me, sending shivers through my body.

I wasn't sure how to take his featherlike touches. He obviously didn't hate me, but right now, I wasn't sure how he felt. All I knew was the look he had on his face when he walked out of the inn. It was an expression that was burned in my mind.

Penny and Clementine were gone. I wasn't sure what Clementine had in mind, and I was a little scared what she would say to my mom, but that worry only lasted for a few moments. I had my own very real issue walking next to me.

"I met Collette when I was a freshman in college." Archer's voice startled me, and I jumped slightly as I turned to face him. His gaze was downturned, and I could see that his jaw muscles were tight.

Not sure what to say or do, I remained quiet. If he wanted to talk, I wasn't going to stop him.

"We were married, and very soon after, she got pregnant." His voice drifted to a whisper.

I wanted to reach down and take his hand. I wanted to give him all the strength that I could, but I still wasn't sure where we were. So I kept my arms wrapped tightly around my chest to fight the urge to touch him.

"Elise was perfect," he whispered. There was so much feeling and emotion in his voice that it took my breath away.

I could no longer keep walking. I needed to see him. To study him. So I turned and faced him. He stopped walking but remained with his head down and his hands shoved into his front pockets. I watched as his shoulders rose and fell. His eyes drifted closed, and I could see the pain as it flowed through his body.

"I was watching her that night. The night she disappeared. I would have stopped her if I'd known, but I was too selfish. I was too distracted. She was gone in a heartbeat, and I couldn't find her." His voice broke as he covered his face with his hand.

Not wanting to leave him standing there, crumbling before me, I stepped forward and wrapped my arms around his waist. I drew myself close to him and rested my head on his chest. I could hear the thumping of his heart and the depth of his breath.

He was broken, just like me.

He remained still for a moment before he wrapped his arms around me. His strength washed over me and took my breath away. We stood there, wrapped in each other's arms.

He leaned forward, nuzzling my neck. I rose up onto my tiptoes as I slipped my arms from his waist up to his neck. We stood there, breathing in unison and just... feeling.

"It wasn't your fault," I said softly. I pulled back so I could meet his gaze. His eyes remained closed for a moment before he opened them and studied me. There was a desperation in his expression as he looked at me.

I reached up and cradled his cheek with my hand. Tears filled my eyes as I stroked his skin with my thumb. He pressed his hands into my lower back, bringing me closer to him.

"I'm broken," he said. His voice was low and deep. It sent shivers down my back.

I nodded as I lowered my free hand to his chest and spread my fingers out. I could feel his heartbeat. It matched the cadence of my own.

"I am too," I whispered.

"I don't deserve a second chance," he whispered.

I shook my head. "That's not true. Everyone deserves a second chance."

He furrowed his brow as he watched me. I held his gaze. I wanted him to feel the truthfulness of my words.

"Are you okay with an unknown future?" His hand was to my cheek now, and I dropped my hand from his face and leaned into his touch.

I nodded into his palm. "I have to believe that Penny will come around. She'll see the beauty of this place and demand that I never leave it. That Magnolia Inn must stay in our family forever."

Archer chuckled as he bent forward and brushed his lips against mine. "And if she doesn't?" He drew back far enough to study me.

My gaze was hazy as I glanced up. I studied him for a moment before I shrugged. "Then we'll find another way."

Archer held my gaze for a moment before he wrapped both arms around me and lifted me up. I giggled as I glanced down at him. He looked sad but also hopeful— and that was how I felt as well.

Dipping down, I pressed my lips to his. All my fears, all my worries, they all washed away as I remained in Archer's arms. He was the lighthouse in my stormy sea. The anchor to my chaotic life.

Magnolia had changed me in a way I'd never imagined, and to think I was ever going to leave was a joke. If Penny kept to her plan to sell the inn, then I'd find another way to stay.

Magnolia was my home, and Archer was my anchor, and there was no way I was leaving either of them.

Archer lowered my feet to the ground, and we

remained wrapped in each other's arms. We were both searching for the answer that we found in each other.

He was broken. I was broken. And yet, our broken pieces managed to fit together to make a perfect whole.

Together we could conquer anything. Even the pain of a tragic past. With each other, we had the one thing we'd been searching for.

Hope.

Hope in the future. Hope in love. And hope that we were eventually going to heal enough to become new.

———

A Week Later

I took in a deep breath as I approached Penny's door. It was her last day here on Magnolia. She'd decided that fixing her relationship with her daughter was important, so she'd taken the week off to spend time with me.

We worked on the inn together during the day and spent time on Magnolia at night. Things were changing with our relationship—at least they were to me.

We'd managed not to talk about the inn or her plans the entire time. But now, as I stood outside her door, it was the moment of truth. I was holding onto the hope that she'd agree to let me run this place. It was pretty much ready to either open or sell.

I was ridiculously optimistic that she would say open.

Gathering my courage, I raised my hand and knocked

three times. I could hear her shuffling around, and a moment later, she opened the door. Her hair was pulled back into a bun, and she was wearing a Magnolia t-shirt and jeans—something I'd never seen my mother wear. Ever.

"Hey," she said as she stepped away from the door.

I entered cautiously. If she was going to pull the rug out from underneath me, I wanted her to do it quickly. "Everything packed?" I asked.

Penny nodded and punctuated her response with the loud zip of her suitcase. She pulled it off her bed and smiled up at me. "Yes. Although I'm sad to be leaving," she said.

My heart picked up speed as I took her words as a good sign. "You can always come back," I said slowly.

Penny eyed me as she passed by me. I was hoping for some hint to what she was thinking, but in true Penny form, there was nothing there. She was as stoic as ever.

"My taxi should be here soon. Walk me to the door?" she asked.

I nodded and followed her down the stairs. My entire mind was swirling with what was going to happen. Even though Archer and I were officially dating—and nothing was going to change that—I still wanted to plan for my future. With the fate of the inn up in the air, that was impossible to do.

We stood on the porch together. Penny had her hand over her eyes, and she was studying the road, watching for her ride. I studied her, wondering how she could be so quiet when I felt like I was bursting inside.

"Tessa is going to stop by later this week," she said.

My heart sank at that sentence. I swallowed as emotions coated my throat. If Tessa was stopping by, that meant only one thing—Penny was selling.

"Oh. Okay," I said softly.

Penny turned to study me. Slowly a smile spread across her lips. "She's just coming to gather the *For Sale* signs."

I stared at Penny. "I'm sorry, what?"

She reached out and pulled me into a hug. "I'm not selling, Maggie," she whispered.

I was in shock. I couldn't move my body as I stood there, hoping with all hope that what she said was true. "You're not?" I asked.

Penny pulled back, tears clinging to her eyelashes. "No. I can't. Not when this place means so much to you…and to me. We are keeping this for a long time to come."

When the shock wore off, I pulled Penny back for a hug. I hadn't felt this happy—this complete—in a long time. "Thank you," I said softly.

Penny chuckled as she pulled back. "Thank you. You've done a wonderful job here. This place is back to its former beauty." She reached out and patted my hand. "You should be proud of yourself."

I nodded, and even though the shock of suddenly becoming an inn owner left me shaking, I knew I was up to the challenge. "Thanks for believing in me and trusting me."

Penny smiled. "Of course. I've always believed in you." Then she leaned forward. "Now go get that hunky guy and offer him a job as the maintenance man." She winked. "I'll fund your needs until you get up and running. After that, I expect twenty percent of the profits."

I pinched my lips together and nodded. Just before I spoke, a car pulled into the parking lot. Penny gave me a warm smile. "And I always expect a bed to be ready for me when I come."

I nodded again, this time, a tear slipping down my cheek. It was as if all the broken pieces inside of me were shifting back into place and my body couldn't contain the completeness that I felt. "Of course."

"I'll call you when I get home. Keep me updated on the official opening."

I nodded and watched as Penny descended the stairs and walked over to the back door of the car. She paused and then turned and waved. I waved back and stood on the porch until her car disappeared into the distance.

With her gone, I hurried back into the house and grabbed my keys and purse. I needed to get to the hardware store to tell Clementine and Archer.

They were just as stressed as I was, and I knew that they were waiting for Penny's answer. My heart was bursting with excitement, and I couldn't wait to tell them.

I was here to stay.

Magnolia was officially my home, and I couldn't wait to get started on the rest of my life.

***

I hope you enjoyed The Magnolia Inn and reading about Maggie finally getting the happily ever after she deserved.

In A Magnolia Homecoming, Jake is back in Magnolia which completely shakes up Clementines world. Plus, something is going on with Shari, and it's up to Clementine and Jake to find out what that is.

Want more of Maggie and Archer? Sign up for my newsletter and get this bonus scene, HERE!

Or use this QR code to grab the bonus scene:

Want more Red Stiletto Bookclub Romances?? Head on over and grab your next read HERE.

For a full reading order of Anne-Marie's books, you can find them HERE.

Or scan below:

Made in the USA
Columbia, SC
19 April 2025

56854957R00171